"Lad . . . whatever I want!"

Sean whirled on Hope, his dark eyes flashing with fury. "You're the one who turned up at my door, spinning a tale that, frankly, only an idiot would believe. But on the strength of this perfectly preposterous story, I've let you go through my father's papers, knowing all the time that if you can find any so-called proof of this loony story of yours, you'll use it to destroy my father's reputation."

Hope was staring at him. "Is *that* what you think?"

"What else is there to think?"

"You could think that I'm right!" Hope said. "Or maybe you already know that I'm right. You say my story is preposterous. It's no more preposterous than expecting me to believe that Whitey Baker's own son never knew about this. Maybe you do know about it, and maybe you don't want the world to know."

Dear Reader,

Once again, Silhouette Intimate Moments is breaking new ground. In our constant search to bring you the best romance fiction in the world, we have found a book that's very different from the usual, and yet it's so appealing and romantic that we just had to publish it. I'm talking about *Angel on my Shoulder,* by Ann Williams. Ann isn't a new author, of course, but the heroine of this book definitely *is* something new. In fact, she's an absolute angel—and I mean that literally! Her name is Cassandra, and she comes to Earth on a mission. Her assignment is to save the soul of one very special man, but she gets a lot more than she bargained for when she takes on an earthly shape—and starts to experience earthly emotions. I don't want to tell you any more for fear of spoiling the magic, so I hope you'll start reading right away and discover for yourself the special nature of this book.

Another book is special to me this month, too, though for a more personal reason. In *The Man Next Door,* author Alexandra Sellers not only creates some very appealing human characters, she introduces some precocious felines, as well. And if you think Lorna Doone and Beetle are too good to be true, I feel honor bound to tell you that they're actually very real. In fact, they're both living in my house, where they're more than willing to cause all sorts of trouble. But now, through the vividness of Alexandra's writing, you can get to know them, too. I hope you like them—as well as *The Man Next Door.*

Marilyn Pappano and Lucy Hamilton, two more of your favorite authors, finish off the month in fine style. And in coming months, look for Kathleen Eagle (back after a long absence), Emilie Richards, Heather Graham Pozzessere, Kathleen Korbel, Jennifer Greene and more of the top-notch writers who have made Silhouette Intimate Moments such a reader favorite.

Enjoy!

Leslie Wainger
Senior Editor and Editorial Coordinator

LUCY HAMILTON

Taking Sides

SILHOUETTE·INTIMATE·MOMENTS®

Published by Silhouette Books New York

America's Publisher of Contemporary Romance

 **SILHOUETTE BOOKS**
300 East 42nd St., New York, N.Y. 10017

TAKING SIDES

ISBN: 0-373-07407-7

First Silhouette Books printing November 1991

Books by Lucy Hamilton

Silhouette Special Edition

A Woman's Place #18
All's Fair #92
Shooting Star #172
The Bitter with the Sweet #206
An Unexpected Pleasure #337

Silhouette Intimate Moments

Agent Provocateur #126
Under Suspicion #229
After Midnight #237
Heartbeats #245
The Real Thing #278
Emma's War #331
Taking Sides #407

*Dodd Memorial Hospital Trilogy

LUCY HAMILTON

traces her love of books to her childhood, and her love of writing to her college days. Her training and the years she spent as a medical librarian translated readily into a career as a writer. "I didn't realize it until I began to write, but a writer is what I was meant to be." An articulate public speaker, the mother of an active grade-school-age daughter and the wife of a physician, Lucy brings diversity and often an extensive knowledge of the medical community to her writing. Although she has now returned to her native Indiana, she often sets her books in Southern California, her home of many years.

To Pat Teal,
who really went through a lot with this one!
Thank you, Pat, for everything.

Chapter 1

" . . . And it's another hot, smoggy day in L.A., folks. Typical September weather, with highs in the upper nineties downtown, about a hundred and seven in the Valley and near ninety at the beaches. Take it easy out there, folks, and go to the beach if you can."

"I wish I could," Hope Carruthers muttered, and switched off the radio. It was 11:00 a.m. and already scorching heat was shimmering up from the pavement in baking waves. Hope braked to a stop as a traffic light changed to red, blotted a trickle of sweat from her temple and wished, not for the first time, that the air-conditioning in her twenty-year-old station wagon still worked.

Of course, if it did, she wouldn't be able to afford the extra gasoline to run it. Her old monster of a wagon, with its V-8 engine, was murder on the mileage even without air-conditioning. It was transportation, though, and it was transportation she needed today.

Hope glanced down at the newspaper, reading, for about the thousandth time, the headline that had blared up at her from Sunday's entertainment section. *The Whitey Baker Story!* it shouted. *Scandalous Secrets, or the Same Old Stuff?*

In most cities, entertainment news and "hard" news were very different things. In L.A., entertainment news *was* hard news. Anything to do with film, television and the entertainment industry was reported in detail from an industry insider's viewpoint. In the ten months she'd been here, Hope had dutifully read the *Times* entertainment section from cover to cover every day, seeking any mention of the name she was interested in. She'd become discouraged almost to the point of giving up as the weeks passed, and then the months, with no mention at all of one of the legends of Hollywood's golden age.

Hope had grown up on her father's stories of Whitey Baker, the millionaire producer and screenwriter who was responsible for some of Hollywood's greatest epics. She'd expected that when she finally arrived in Los Angeles, she'd have no trouble learning everything she needed to know about the famous man.

The trouble was, she found when she got to L.A., Whitey Baker had died over ten years ago. Ten years was an eternity in Hollywood, where someone new was hot each week, where "legends" were made, and then forgotten, from month to month. Whitey Baker was old news, the subject of an occasional retrospective film festival at UCLA, admired but largely forgotten. He certainly didn't make the papers.

Until last Sunday, three days ago. Hope had been flipping through the sections, idly reading headlines, when she'd seen that name. She'd frozen, the newspa-

per dropping from her nerveless hands, the fat sections
scattering around her feet. She scrabbled feverishly
among them until she found the one she wanted, and
devoured the article while standing in her front doorway.

A deal had been struck, she read, for a biography of
Whitey Baker. Actually, it was to be "the definitive biography of a flamboyant filmmaker who remains an
enigma to most," according to the publishing house vice
president who had persuaded Whitey Baker's son to
write the story of his father's life.

His son! Hope had been both astonished and elated.
She'd vaguely remembered being told that Whitey had
a little boy named Sean, but when she tried to locate
him, she'd been looking for Sean Baker. She'd never
known that Whitey's name was actually Boudreaux,
changed to the more English-sounding Baker when he
came to Hollywood from Chicago in the late twenties.
The information in that newspaper article had enabled
her, after three days of intense searching, to locate the
address of Sean Boudreaux, and now she was on her
way to talk to him.

The light changed, the car in front of her moved off,
and she hauled the station wagon around the sharp right
turn and up the first hill in a steeply winding canyon
road.

She'd found this road on the map and wondered if
anything navigable could really be as twisty and winding as that fine blue line leading to Sean Boudreaux's
address. It was, if anything, worse than the blue line on
the map, for the road itself clung precariously to the
hillside, with houses on the cliff above it on the right,
and clinging to the precipitous hill below it on the left.
The terrain was so steep that most were invisible from

the level of the road, save for mailboxes and drive-
ways. Hope got an uneasy feeling in the pit of her
stomach each time she swung her big car around another tight, narrow turn. She didn't shoot off into
space, but she couldn't quite get rid of the feeling that
she might.

She was frankly relieved to finally see the number she
was looking for on a large, plain, galvanized mailbox on
the uphill side of the road, just around one of the most
hair-raising of the bends. Her engine protested as she
started up the steep grade of the drive, which twisted
sharply to the right, then left, then right again, before
it leveled off suddenly into a wide parking circle with a
fountain playing in the center.

"Wow!" Hope braked to a stop beside the fountain,
staring in wonder at the house that faced her. It was a
mansion straight out of a Busby Berkeley fantasy, and
though she'd seen a picture of it, the grainy black-and-
white newspaper photo hadn't done justice to the reality. Built in the 1930s, it was a Spanish-Southwest fantasy in creamy stucco and red tile, trimmed with
wrought iron and frosted in flowering vines. It reminded Hope of nothing so much as a gigantic cup-
cake.

The man who'd owned this house had been rich. Not
just sort of rich, but really, truly, Hollywood-in-the-
forties-and-fifties filthy rich. His son, whom Hope had
come to see, still lived here. Though the son reportedly
avoided the fast-track life-style his father had become
famous for, he must be wealthy, too, if he could afford
even the upkeep on a house like this. The rich son of a
very famous man—she wondered how he'd react to
what she had to say.

The question made her nervous, but she wasn't about to back out now. She'd had to wait three long days since she saw that newspaper article and the way to finally make her dream a reality. This meeting meant everything to her, and it was too important to be bungled.

In a gesture of bravado, Hope parked her shabby station wagon smack in front of the spectacular house and marched boldly up the flight of marble steps leading to the massive, iron-studded front door. Predictably enough, there was a big iron door knocker in the shape of a clenched fist. Hope shook her head in amusement at the knocker, but rather than pound that iron fist on the door, she searched until she found a bell embedded in the ironwork beside the door.

She pressed it, and her grin widened as several bars of Big Ben's chimes pealed sonorously in the distance. It would have been a big disappointment if the doorbell on *this* house had been a simple ding-dong.

The chimes died away, and though she waited for several long minutes, nothing happened until the sprinklers on the lawn suddenly came on with a whirr and clatter. Hope turned away from the door to watch the spray of droplets, like diamonds in the sunlight.

"What is it?"

The demand came from the doorway behind her, irritable and abrupt. Hope jumped and whirled around, a hand to her throat.

"Miss?" A tall, obviously annoyed man scowled down at her from the doorway. "What do you want?"

Hope just stared at him. She had no idea what he thought when he looked at her, but on first seeing him, her only thought was tall, dark and handsome. Sean Boudreaux fit the stereotype perfectly.

He was tall, at least an inch or so over six feet. And he was dark with wavy, jet-black hair cut fashionably short and brushed straight back from his face, and the kind of smooth, olive-toned skin that takes the sun easily and evenly. And handsome? Even seen through her sunglasses, he was startlingly handsome, with a lean, muscular build and a face that belonged on a movie screen. His eyes were such a dark brown they were nearly black, deep set beneath straight brows; his cheekbones were high and his nose was narrow and straight and just slightly aquiline. His jaw was square, with a slight cleft in his chin, and his mouth...

"Miss?" he repeated. "Is there something you want?"

Hope blinked. "Ah...yes," she stammered. "Y-yes, there is. Is..." She took one deep breath. "Are you Sean Boudreaux?"

"Yes."

"And was the man who went by the name Whitey Baker your father?"

He didn't answer the question. Instead, his unwavering regard sharpened suddenly into suspicion. "Are you a reporter?"

"What?" Jolted out of her catechism by the question, Hope frowned.

"Are you a reporter?"

"A reporter?" She, who would have had nothing to do with a reporter for any reason? Hope almost laughed at the idea. "Of course not!"

"Then what are you?"

"I'm a second-grade teacher," she told him.

"A teacher?" he repeated, incredulous.

"Yes. Second grade."

He shook his head, then frowned. "Then why are you asking all these questions?"

"I have a good reason," she told him. "*Was* your father Whitey Baker?"

He hesitated for a long moment, while the sprinklers chattered and a car whooshed by on the road below them. "Yes," Sean Boudreaux admitted at last. "He used the name Whitey Baker."

She nodded. "In that case, Mr. Boudreaux, I need to talk to you."

They faced each other in silence for several seconds. His frown deepened. "About my father?"

"Yes."

"You're not a reporter?"

"No, I'm not."

He frowned, lips thinned in concentration. "What's your connection with my father?"

"Could I explain about that inside, Mr. Boudreaux? It's awfully hot out here."

His glance flicked from the perspiration beaded at her temples to the damp sheen of her throat, and after a moment he gave a curt nod. "Come in." He stepped back, pulling the door wide.

Hope followed him into a dim, blissfully cool entry hall, pulled off her sunglasses and gazed around her in awe. The ceiling soared two and a half stories above the flagstone floor, while whitewashed stucco walls curved around a wide sweep of stone staircase lifting toward the second floor.

When she turned, sunglasses in hand, and looked up at Sean Boudreaux, she was smiling at the sheer, unabashed, ostentatious majesty of it.

And it was his turn to stare at her, his eyes widening as they met hers. Hope didn't know why he was staring, but it made her uncomfortable, for she wasn't used to being stared at. She knew perfectly well she didn't fit the blond, tanned mold of California-surfer beauty.

She was too pale, too brunette, too un-Californian. Instead of skin that tanned to a luscious gold and hair the color of ripe wheat, she had fair skin that reddened in the sun—before it freckled—and an unruly mass of near-black curls that fell well below her shoulders and defied her best efforts to tame it.

She wasn't tall or athletic, either. She was only five foot three, not quite average, if you believed the actuarial tables, and if she was athletic, she'd never shown any signs of it. When she'd still been in convent school, Sister Costanza, the phys ed teacher, had despaired of her at volleyball, field hockey, tennis, gymnastics and softball. The only thing she seemed able to do was swim, and she wasn't an athlete even at that. Sister Costanza, despite her determination, had finally given up.

She didn't even have the blue eyes that all California girls were supposed to have. She returned Sean Boudreaux's gaze for a moment with her non-Californian green eyes, then said, to break the lengthening silence, "Your home is lovely."

Sean blinked, as if coming out of a trance. "It was my father's," he replied distractedly. "He built it." He looked around. "It's not exactly my style, but he wanted me to have it, so..." He cleared his throat. "Would you like something to drink? Coffee or a soda?"

"Thank you," Hope replied politely. "A soda would be nice."

"Okay. A soda. Yeah." He stepped back and indicated a wide, arched doorway on the right. "The living room's through there. Make yourself comfortable. I'll only be a minute."

"Thank you." He waited until she started toward the archway before he moved away, toward the rear of the house. Alone, Hope walked slowly into the huge living room. It was as dramatic as the outside of the house, with a vast stone fireplace at one end and french windows lining the longest wall, facing east. Hope ignored the antique chairs and sofas positioned around the room and walked across to the windows, to stand gazing out at the view of canyon and mountains.

"I didn't know whether you'd rather have cola or ginger ale, so I brought both."

Hope jumped when he spoke from just behind her, for she hadn't heard him coming.

"Cola is fine," she said, her voice just a little too high. She cleared her throat. "You have a magnificent view."

"I'm glad you like it." He set a tray on one of the low tables and poured cola over ice in a glass. "Here you are."

"Thank you." Hope accepted the glass and seated herself on the rose brocade cushions of a graceful Queen Anne love seat.

He took an armchair opposite her. "You have the advantage of me."

"I beg your pardon?"

"You know my name, but I don't know yours."

"Oh, I see. My name is Carruthers, Mr. Boudreaux. Hope Carruthers." She watched his face closely but saw no flicker of reaction to her name.

"I'm pleased to meet you, Ms. Carruthers." He extended his hand, and Hope reached out to shake it briefly.

She almost snatched it away the moment they touched. The moment of contact was startling, like touching an electric wire. His hand was big and warm, enfolding hers in a grip that was gentle but held the promise of strength. When she pulled away, sitting very straight and stiff on the brocade cushions, she pressed her hand into the folds of her cotton skirt as if to hide it from him. With her fist clenched in her lap she could still feel his big hand engulfing her smaller one.

He took a sip of his own soda, then leaned forward, his gaze fixed on her face. "Now, Ms. Carruthers, let's get to the business at hand. What's with all the questions about my father? And why are you here?"

Hope looked up from her glass and found that his gaze, fixed on her, was noticeably cooler than before. She met his eyes with a cool, level gaze of her own.

"My name is Hope Carruthers," she told him again. "Are you sure that doesn't mean anything to you?"

"Should it?"

"I thought it might. It would have meant something to your father."

"To Whitey?" His frown deepened. "Why should your name mean anything to him?"

She didn't answer that question. "I read in the newspaper that you're going to write a book about him, his biography."

"That's right. But what does a biography of Whitey Baker have to do with you?" He regarded her levelly, then smiled, some secret joke lighting his dark, dark eyes. "Unless you're a long-lost heir, come to claim your rightful place, not to mention your inheritance? As far as I know I'm his only child, but as many times as Whitey was married and divorced, an unknown daughter certainly wouldn't be impossible!"

Hope had to laugh at that. "You don't need to worry, Mr. Boudreaux. I'm definitely not Whitey Baker's long-lost child. That's not why I've come." Suddenly nervous, she rose and walked a few feet away, standing with her back to him, looking out the windows again.

He let the silence stretch for a moment. "You know, I'm getting a little tired of asking the same thing over and over. Why have you come here?"

Hope took a deep breath and turned to face him. "Because of the biography," she said. "The one you're going to write about your father. You'll be writing about his career, won't you, about the movies he produced and the screenplays he wrote?" She turned to watch his face as he replied.

"Of course I'll be writing about his movies. His career was the biggest part of his life, after all. His work and his movies will be half the book."

"Which movies?" she asked quickly. "*The Centurion*? *Six Plus Three*? *Desert Heat*?"

"Yes," he replied, puzzled. "Those and all the others."

"But you can't write about them." She took a step toward him. "Not those movies, and not the others that he didn't write."

"*What?*" He rose slowly from his chair, staring across the short distance that separated them. "What the *hell* are you talking about?"

"About the screenplays," she told him, her tone making it clear the answer should have been obvious. "It's important that you write about the movies he wrote, but of course you can't write about the ones he didn't write."

"What do you mean, the ones he didn't write?" Sean crossed the distance to her in a couple of long strides and caught her arms in a grip that hurt. "Tell me what you're talking about!"

"I'm talking about the screenplays!" She jerked free of his hands and glared up at him. "About the ones my father wrote, that your father sold."

"You're crazy!" he snapped.

"No, I'm not! You know perfectly well what I'm talking about! My father was Philip Carruthers."

He just shook his head. "I told you before, I don't know anyone named Carruthers."

"Your father did."

Hope watched his face, waiting for the suspicion to ease, the implacability to soften. It didn't, but after a moment he nodded, one curt nod.

"Tell me."

"Philip Carruthers was my father," she repeated. "His best friend in the world was Whitey Baker—your father. They were close, closer than brothers in a lot of ways."

"Carruthers." Sean half turned away, running a hand over his face. "Carruthers. Maybe I have heard the name, maybe when I was a kid, but... Wait a minute!" He looked around at her. "Was he a screenwriter, like my dad? In the forties?"

"The forties and fifties," she told him. "He left the country, with my mother, in August of 1951. He was blacklisted, and then he was subpoenaed, and they went to Mexico."

Sean swore under his breath, short and sharp.

"That's one way of putting it." Hope's lips twisted in a small, bitter smile. "He was a busy writer in the forties, well respected. He was nominated for an Oscar in 1947, and he was considered one of the best. Then Joe McCarthy came along, and HUAC and the witch-hunts. He'd joined the Communist Party in college, in the late thirties, in the same way other students joined clubs or fraternities. I don't think the party ever meant more to him than a social club that would raise a few eyebrows, but he was a member, and he stayed a member, and that fact destroyed him."

"What happened?"

Hope shrugged. "The same thing that happened to so many. He was blacklisted and he lost everything. First he lost his job, and then he lost the house in Toluca Lake, and then he lost his country. He took my mother and went to Mexico rather than answer the subpoena and be jailed for refusing to testify. He might never have considered the party more than a club, but he would never have testified against others. He would never have named names."

She turned away again, leaning on a chair back as she gazed blindly out the window. "After he went to Mexico, his reputation was destroyed, shredded in the American press. He read the newspapers and the magazines, and each article was another knife in his heart. And then my mother died."

"Where were you all this time?"

"I was born in Mexico City. My mother was forty-three when she became pregnant, and she'd contracted tuberculosis as a child. She was never strong, and pregnancy and childbirth were too much for her. When I was six months old she died, leaving my father alone in exile with a baby to raise."

"So he'd lost everything," Sean said.

"Almost everything. He still had a friend." Hope looked over her shoulder at him. "Whitey Baker. Your father."

"My father, the screenwriter."

"Exactly," she agreed. "Just as my father was a screenwriter. But my father was blacklisted. He couldn't work, not openly at any rate. And since he couldn't sell his screenplays, his very good friend—"

"Whitey Baker."

She nodded. "His friend Whitey Baker helped him. If it weren't for Whitey, my father would have been destitute. What he did . . ." She paused, biting her lip.

"What *did* he do?" Sean prompted.

"He sold my father's scripts as his own," she said quietly. "They made an agreement. Surely you know about the agreement?" she appealed to him.

He shook his head, and after a moment she went on.

"Philip, my father, kept writing while he was living in Mexico. He sent the scripts to Whitey. Whitey sold them under his own name and sent the money back to Philip in Mexico."

Several seconds ticked past while Sean stared at her. "You have *got* to be kidding."

"I'm not. You know I'm not."

"I don't know anything of the kind." He stalked several steps away, then wheeled around. "I do know that this whole story is ridiculous. It's too farfetched. You can't expect me to take it seriously."

"I've never been more serious in my life." Hope lifted her chin. "My father was ill for a long time, and he died less than a year ago. At first I didn't know what I could do to honor his memory, but I've figured it out. I'm going to see that Philip Carruthers's movies are properly credited to him."

"Are you *nuts?*" he demanded. "You want to credit my father's work to someone I've barely heard of?"

"To the man who actually wrote that work. To the man who was your father's friend."

"Yeah, right. And since your father was such a great friend of mine, you want to tell the world that my father didn't write his own movies? No way!"

"Look, Mr. Boudreaux," she appealed to him, her hands outstretched. "I don't want to hurt your father's memory. After what your father did for mine, I'd never do that. But I have to see that the truth is told."

"You could hardly damage my father's personal reputation," Sean said dryly. "Any man who had five wives has little enough reputation left anyway. I've never been impressed by the way he led his life, but about his work..." He walked slowly back to Hope, watching her intently, searching her face for the truth, when he stopped an arm's length away. "Do you really believe this nonsense?"

"I don't have to believe it. I know it, because it's true."

He stared at her for several seconds more, than shook his head. "So what do you propose to do? Take this crazy story of yours and go to the press?"

"Of course not! Nobody would believe it on my word alone. You certainly don't." She shot him a speaking look, but Sean didn't flinch. "I have to have proof to take them. Convincing proof. I already have some evidence, but I'll need more. That's why I've come to you."

Sean frowned. "Now I'm really confused. I thought you came here to tell me not to write my book."

"I'd like you to write the truth in your book. I'd like nothing better. There's no reason I should tell you not to write it," she told him reasonably. "I came here this morning to tell you what I'm going to do, because you have a right to know."

"Oh, gee, it's really swell of you to admit that," he murmured in a sarcastic undertone.

Hope ignored the sarcasm. "And I came for the rest of the proof."

"You came to *me* for proof of this story of yours?"

"That's right."

"But why should I give you *anything,* much less this purported evidence?"

"Because you're writing his biography. I assume you're writing the truth."

"I am." His voice was cold.

"Then you're the only person who would have it. The only place the rest of the evidence I need could be is in Whitey's papers. You're his heir, so I assume you have his papers."

"I have his papers," he admitted grudgingly.

"Then you have the rest of the proof," she concluded on a note of triumph.

Sean raked a hand through his hair in frustrated annoyance. "This is getting weirder and weirder. You keep saying 'the rest of the proof.' What 'proof' do you have?"

"Letters, and my father's notebook."

"Did you bring them with you?" he snapped.

"No." She shrugged. "I didn't think I'd need to. I thought you'd know about the agreement."

"Well, I don't. Where are these things you have?"

"They're put away safely. At home."

"I want to see them."

"All right." She saw no reason not to agree. "You have a right to see them."

"They're at your place, you say?"

She nodded again. "I have them put away, safe."

"Fine. I have a meeting I can't get out of today, but I can wind that up by five or so. I'll come by your place afterward to see the stuff." He stepped closer as he spoke, until he seemed to be looming over her, too big and overwhelming for comfort.

Hope felt a surge of panic. "I don't . . . I don't think that's a good idea," she said hastily.

"Why?" he demanded. "Do you have something planned for tonight? Won't you be home?"

Hope racked her brain for a quick answer. She wasn't sure why, but she didn't want Sean Boudreaux at her house. He intimidated her, and having him in her home would be almost an invasion. "I'll—uh—I'll be out most of the day," she stammered. That wasn't true— she'd taken the day off to handle this—but he wouldn't know that. "It would be easier if we met somewhere."

"Okay." He thought about that for a moment. "What part of town will you be in? We can meet somewhere close."

"I'll be in the Valley," she told him. "Northridge."

"I know a good place in Encino. You like Italian?"

Hope nodded. Everybody liked spaghetti.

"Good. I'll meet you at—say—seven?"

"Seven will be fine."

He nodded. "All right, we'll meet at seven." He told her the name of the restaurant and its address. "You'll bring those papers you have?"

"I'll bring them."

Chapter 2

Sean was confused.

A morning that had started like any other, with coffee and a run along the canyon, had suddenly lurched off-kilter. He'd been peacefully working in his study when that crazy baroque doorbell of Whitey's had gone off and shattered far more than the peaceful morning.

Who was Hope Carruthers and where on earth had she come from?

Philip Carruthers. Though the name had finally rung a bell for Sean, it was an awfully faint bell. If he hadn't spent his early life surrounded by the actors, directors and screenwriters who were Whitey's friends, he might never have heard the name Carruthers.

And this girl said she was Philip Carruthers's daughter. Well, there was no reason why she shouldn't be, he supposed. But she'd better have a darned good reason for turning up on his doorstep saying that Whitey Baker didn't write the screenplay for *The Centurion*! She must be crazy!

She didn't look crazy. He tilted his big desk chair back and swiveled around to look at the view of the canyon out his study window. No, despite the crazy assertions she was flinging around, she didn't look crazy.

She looked determined. And scared. Partly scared, partly belligerent, and awfully young for her age. If the dates she'd given him were correct, she had to be in her late twenties by now, but she looked years younger.

And she was beautiful.

At first sight, she'd reminded him of a heroine from some nineteenth-century novel. She was small, not much more than five-three or so, and slender, fine-boned. Dressed in a skirt of some lightweight floaty material and a round-necked blouse, with flat shoes and her sable curls tied back in a girlish ribbon, she'd looked not quite real, as if he had found Alice in Wonderland on his Los Angeles doorstep. Unlikely, to say the least.

She'd looked nervous when he'd answered the door. He remembered the spasm of nerves he'd seen in her face before she stiffened her spine and began hurling questions at him.

But what a face. It was a face out of a painting, oval and creamy-skinned, with a flush of rose on the fine cheekbones, soft, unpainted pink lips and thick, dark lashes around eyes as green as the hills of Ireland.

And those eyes! Sean could still see them. Green eyes were always striking, but hers were mysterious, almost magical. A true, deep green, they held no hint of hazel but had flecks of gold, like fire lurking deep within.

That fire had flashed quick and hot when she sprang to her father's defense, making a mockery of her initially shy, hesitant manner. She might dress like a ro-

mantic ingenue, but there was passion in her soul. He
had heard it in her voice and seen it in her eyes when she
sprang to the defense of her father and his work.

Sean could only envy someone who felt such clear-cut
emotion for a parent. His feelings about his own father
and mother were far too complicated and problematic
to be reduced to the simplicity of Hope Carruthers's
feelings for Philip. It wasn't until he was an adult that
Sean had finally reached an uneasy truce with his Florida socialite mother, a truce made possible by the fact
that they kept a continent's distance between them for
most of the year, limiting visits to a couple of duty-day
holidays each year.

His feelings for his father were even more muddied
and complicated. Even now, years after Whitey's death,
Sean hadn't sorted through the confused welter of resentment, love, anger, admiration and jealousy that
colored his memories of his father.

It was that fact that had convinced him to write
Whitey's biography. He didn't feel uncomplicated ad-
oration for his father any more than he felt pure ha-
tred. There were things that Sean despised about Whitey
Baker and the life he'd led, and there were things he
admired, and just maybe, by writing the man's life
story, he could sort it all out.

He didn't know what to make of Hope Carruthers's
nutty story about scripts and blacklisted writers and his
father's work, but he knew he couldn't ignore her allegations. He'd get more information from her tonight,
and maybe he could sort out her story. And even if he
couldn't solve the mystery, he was having dinner with a
beautiful girl who undeniably intrigued him.

A smile tugged at Sean's lips. He was looking forward to dinner at seven.

* * *

Hope perched tensely on the edge of a red velveteen chair in the restaurant lobby and tried not to look nervous. She'd expected an Italian restaurant like the one near the convent in Mexico City. She'd expected a small, plain, cheerful place with red-checked table-cloths and candles stuck in bottles.

This was something else entirely. She'd been met at the curb by a young man who insisted on parking her car, then greeted at the door by a maître d' who wanted to know how many were in her party. She'd accepted his invitation to wait in the plush lobby for Sean, and accepted a glass of mineral water with lime from an attentive waiter.

They were all perfectly pleasant and polite, but she knew, and she knew they knew, that she was out of her element here.

She'd never in her life been in a restaurant like this. The lobby she waited in was opulently decorated in red velvet and oriental rugs, sparkling with brass and crystal light fixtures. The soft sounds of a jazz trio drifted from the lounge, and through a wide archway she could see the dining room, with snowy tablecloths and sparkling chandeliers, candles and flowers on every table.

Hope glanced around her again, then dropped her gaze to the envelope she clutched in her lap. She wasn't used to a place like this, and she wasn't dressed for it, either. Her dress was hopelessly old-fashioned, a flowered cotton with a skirt that floated nearly to her ankles. It was all wrong for this restaurant. No one else in this place was wearing floaty florals. No one else was nervous.

Everyone else in the restaurant was accustomed to places with valet parking and tuxedoed headwaiters.

Everyone else fit in. The closest Hope had ever come to something like this was seeing it in the movies.

Her upbringing had included a good academic education, rigorous religious training and a solid grounding in etiquette, but since arriving in L.A. ten months ago, she'd come to realize that there were some big gaps in all that education. She'd been a little too protected for a little too long, and she still had a lot to learn.

She hoped she would prove a quick study. As things stood now, she was at a definite disadvantage with a sophisticated man like Sean Boudreaux.

She glanced at her watch. Six fifty-seven. The virtues of punctuality having been drummed into her from childhood, she'd arrived fifteen minutes early. Now she was beginning to wonder if she shouldn't have chosen to arrive "fashionably late" rather than endure this nerve-racking wait.

She glanced around her again, meeting the gaze of a very thin, very tanned woman of forty-something, dressed in high, high heels, skinny knit leggings and a voluminous silk tunic with an appliqué of a fantastic peacock on the front. The woman looked Hope up and down and smiled in supercilious amusement. A little surge of anger went through Hope, and she lifted her chin defiantly, staring back until the peacock woman flushed beneath her heavy makeup and looked away.

The peacock woman had a short, jagged, geometric haircut. Hope tucked a stray curl back into the knot she'd coiled on her nape and looked down at her hands again, wishing futilely that she had skinny leggings and a silk tunic and nerve enough to wear them to dinner at a restaurant.

"The young lady is waiting in the lobby, sir," the maître d' told him.

Sean saw her as soon as he reached the wide archway leading to the lobby area. She was unmistakable, even with her back to him, a drift of pastel amid the strong, acid colors that seemed to be this season's latest thing. She looked fresh and cool and sweet, like peach ice cream on a summer day. Sean was smiling as he threaded his way across the crowded room to her.

"Hope." He was standing behind her when he spoke, and she jumped like a startled rabbit. She was holding a glass of something, and when she jumped, it slipped from her hand.

Sean grabbed for the glass, too late, and together they watched—Hope in horror, Sean in amusement—as soda and ice and the little wedge of lime splattered on the deep red carpet.

"Oh, no!" Hope's gasp was ripe with despair.

Sean caught her arm before she could stoop to sop at the spill with a handful of tissues from her purse, and kept her standing beside him as he signaled a hovering waiter.

"I'm so sorry," Hope whispered as the waiter hurried across with napkins and a tray. "I'm terribly sorry," she told him in an agony of embarrassment.

The waiter grinned reassurance. "No problem, miss. It happens all the time." He quickly finished his mopping up and departed with another smile, a tray of wet napkins and a discreet tip from Sean.

Though the waiter carried away the evidence of the spill, he couldn't take Hope's embarrassment with him. Even in the dimly lighted lobby, Sean could see that her cheeks were burning. She wouldn't look up at him but glanced furtively at an overdressed matron with a peacock on her shirt. The peacock woman smirked and said something to her escort that made him glance around. The woman looked toward Hope again, but Sean caught her eye. Her eyes widened at the look on his face, the smirk left her lips, and she turned quickly away.

Satisfied, he bent a little to look into Hope's face. "Are you okay?"

"Me? Of course I am." Shot shot him a quick glance. "After all, you can't actually die of embarrassment, can you?"

"No, you can't," he agreed, amused. "But there's no point in being embarrassed. There's not another person in this place who's worried about that spilled glass of soda. See?"

At his urging, she risked a glance around them. It was true. No one was looking at her, not even the peacock lady, who was talking very intently with her stout, balding escort. No one else cared at all.

She sighed ruefully. "You're right, I know. One's own mistakes always feel bigger than anyone else's."

"Always." Sean was determined to make her smile, one way or another. "If it'll make you feel any better, though, I can always spill my wine or knock my plate on the floor."

His tired little joke worked. She chuckled, a warm bubble of laughter that made him want to laugh along with her. "I don't think that'll be necessary."

"I'm relieved to hear it." Sean mimed wiping his brow. "I think we can go in now. Are you hungry?"

"Truly?" Hope tipped her head and slanted him a laughing glance. "I'm starving!"

For a moment time stopped. Sean couldn't look away from her eyes, glowing with laughter, warm and emerald and beautiful enough to mesmerize a man. He shook his head a fraction, as if actual physical motion were needed to break the spell. He straightened and stepped back, turning to signal the headwaiter.

Sean had asked for a quiet table, and the maître d' led them to the far side of the large dining room. Hope threaded her way gracefully through the crowd, her flowery skirt swaying with her walk, but when they reached the table, she seemed flustered by the maître d's attentions as he pulled out her chair, shook a heavy linen napkin out across her lap and handed her an opened menu. Sean could see the rosy flush on her cheeks when the maître d' finally departed, and he smiled as Hope hid her face behind her menu.

He studied the top of her head for a moment. "Hope?"

"Yes?" She peered over the top of her menu.

"How old are you?"

She lifted her head at that. "I'm twenty-eight. Why?"

"I just wondered," Sean replied easily. "If our fathers were friends, they must have been fairly close in age, but you're eight years younger than I am."

"They were nearly the same age. My father was a year younger than yours, but he was forty-six when I was born."

"I see." Sean nodded and opened his menu. "Do you see anything you'd like to try?"

She scanned the long columns, then shrugged helplessly. "There's too much to choose from," she admitted. "I don't know where to start. What do you recommend?"

He suggested several things, she chose a veal dish, and they were treated to delicious food and efficient, unobtrusive service. Sean didn't talk much during the meal, content to eat his calamari and study the young woman who had barged into his life.

She was an odd mixture of contradictions. Brave enough to march into his home and hurl a raft of cockamamy theories at him this morning, she now perched tensely on her chair, sneaking looks around her as if she'd never been in a restaurant before. The only thing they were served that she seemed to recognize was the little dish of spumoni ice cream that came with the coffee.

The more he saw of her, the more questions Sean had about her, but he could be patient. He could wait for answers to some of his questions, but he'd have those answers, and more, sooner or later.

"There's a lounge," he said when he'd dealt smoothly with the check. "It might be more comfortable than the dining room. Would you mind if we have our talk there?"

She'd relaxed a little over the excellent food, but Sean could see her tension return when he brought up the reason for this dinner. She'd set the crumpled manila envelope aside while she ate, but when he spoke, she quickly picked it up. "No," she said. "I don't mind."

She clutched the envelope in both hands as he ushered her to a quiet table in the lounge, and held it on her lap while their drinks were served. Sean had brandy; Hope had soda. Was she afraid of alcohol loosening her tongue? he wondered. Or just afraid?

He looked up when the trio began playing across the room. The song was something with a Latin beat, and a few couples were already on the small dance floor.

Hope was watching, too. She turned to Sean, eyes wide. "Do you know what that—uh—dance is that they're doing?"

He looked back at the floor, where the dancers, bodies pressed tightly together, were gyrating in time to the music. "It's called the lambada. I think the fad started in Brazil."

"In Brazil," she repeated, and averted her gaze from the dancers. "I see."

"Would you like to dance?" Sean asked.

Hope recoiled. "N-no. No, thank you!"

Was it him she was afraid of, Sean wondered, or the exhibitionistic lambada? He hid a grin.

"We don't need to do the lambada," he reassured her. "A nice sedate cha-cha would go fine with this song."

Hope ducked her head, and after a moment Sean reached out to lift her face with a fingertip beneath her chin.

"Hey, what's the matter? If you don't like the cha-cha, just say so, okay?"

She shook her head, one stray dark curl brushing her cheek.

Sean gently tucked the curl behind her ear. "If it's not the cha-cha, what is it? What did I say?"

"It's nothing you did." She pulled her chin away from his hand and looked down again. "It's just—I don't know how to dance."

Sean stared. "At all?"

"Not like that." She gestured toward the dance floor. "I know how to waltz. From dances, when I was in school. That's all."

"Waltz?" he repeated. "Where did you go to school?"

"Our Lady of Guadalupe boarding school, outside Mexico City."

"Nuns? Convent school?"

"Mmm-hmm."

"All girls?"

She nodded.

"How many years?"

"Kindergarten through high school, and then Blessed Saint Mary's women's college there."

"More nuns? All girls?" he asked, incredulous.

"Mmm-hmm." She nodded.

"What did you study?"

"Education. I told you I teach. I'm working now at St. Bartholomew's School. It's one of the Order's elementary schools."

"I see. In that case, it's high time to broaden your education." He grabbed her hand and stood, pulling her up with him. "Come on."

Hope wasn't positive she wanted her education broadened *that* much, but she let him pull her onto the dance floor. She stood stiffly while he took her in his arms, her right hand in his, her left resting tentatively on his shoulder. She held her body well away from his and kept her gaze firmly on their feet as she tried to match her steps to his.

"Hope." He lifted her chin with his fingertip again. "This isn't the convent school. The nuns aren't watching you anymore."

"But I don't know the steps."

"Don't worry about steps." He pulled her closer. "Just listen to the music. Relax, feel the beat, and follow me."

He would never know, Hope thought, how difficult it was to relax when Sean Boudreaux was holding her close. He didn't dance the way the boys from the Franciscan Brothers Academy had danced so long ago in Mexico City, with six decorous inches between partners. The boys had asked her only for duty dances, since she wasn't marriage material. The heavily chaperoned dances the nuns sponsored to help the eighteen-year-old daughters of wealthy families catch husbands had been something different for Hope.

She wasn't the highly marriageable daughter of a wealthy family. She was the charity student, the *norteamericana* whose father was *loco*. The boys asked her to dance because the Brothers insisted, but they'd made their disdain clear.

If Sean was feeling any disdain as he danced with her, she couldn't tell it.

He held her lightly but firmly, guiding her movements with the swaying of his body, urging her into the rhythm of the dance. Their knees brushed as they moved, her skirt floated around his legs, and she could feel the muscles flex in his arm around her waist. If they were under the sharp-eyed surveillance of Sister Maria Catalina, she thought, even Sean wouldn't dare hold her so close. Hope chuckled at the idea, and he looked down, smiling.

"Share the joke?"

She tried to stifle a grin. "I was thinking of Sister Maria Catalina. She'd have rapped your knuckles for dancing this way."

"A tough cookie, was she?"

"The toughest."

"I see. Well, what would she have done if I'd danced with you like this?" He closed the last inch of space that separated them, so that their bodies touched from breast to knees, their legs lightly interlaced, the rhythm of their steps hinting at another, much older rhythm. The gauzy fabric of her dress wasn't enough to keep her from feeling the heat of his body, and she knew she was flushing, not from embarrassment but from something else, something new.

"I can't..." She couldn't seem to catch her breath. "I can't even imagine what Sister would do."

"That's okay. Sister isn't here now."

"No," Hope whispered, "she's not."

She knew she ought to push him away, but her brain couldn't quite form the commands, and her muscles wouldn't have obeyed them anyway. It was so easy to relax in his arms, to follow the seductive movements of the dance, to rest her cheek on his shoulder, close her eyes and breathe the faint, intoxicating scent of his after-shave.

"Hope?"

With a start, she opened her eyes. As she came back to reality, she realized the song was over, and the other dancers were drifting back to their tables.

"I thought a dance might help you relax," Sean said as he walked her through the tables, "but I didn't plan on putting you to sleep."

Hope wasn't in the mood for teasing. She stiffened, pulling away from his guiding hand at her waist. "I wasn't asleep," she retorted, embarrassment sharpening her tone, "but do you think we could do the business we came here to do?"

"Certainly we can," he replied with a careful courtesy that pointed up her burst of ill temper. He moved back, taking his hand from her waist, guiding her back to the table without touching her at all. It was almost, Hope thought, as if an invisible wall had sprung up between them.

"I'm sorry," she muttered. "That was rude."

Sean inclined his head in acknowledgement, politely, but with none of the easy warmth that they'd shared only a few minutes earlier.

"Not at all," he said. "You're right. We came here to do some business."

He held her chair for her, then took his own seat while Hope opened the envelope she'd brought. She slid out several crumpled letters and a small dime-store notebook with yellowing pages.

"Here they are." She passed them carefully to Sean.

Without comment, he scanned the letters, then paged through the notebook before placing it all in a neat stack on the table.

"Well?" Hope prompted anxiously.

He shrugged. "What is this supposed to prove?"

"Don't you see?" She opened the notebook to the first page, and pointed to a faded entry scribbled in pencil. "Right here, see? He noted the date he finished the script of *The Centurion*."

Sean looked, then shook his head. "To tell you the truth, I don't *see* much of anything. A date, and the letters *T, C, c.* What's that supposed to mean?"

"That's the shorthand he used, his own sort of code. *TC* stands for *The Centurion*, and the lowercase *c* means it was completed. On the next page is the date he sent it to Whitey."

Sean looked at that, too, shaking his head. "*Christmas minus six, Mo?* What does that have to do with my father?"

"It's code, remember? *Christmas minus six* is the date, December 19, and he called your father *Mo*. Wasn't his given name Maurice?"

"Before he changed it, yeah."

"There it is, then. Mo, for Maurice."

Sean frowned. "So you're saying that these letters from somebody called Mo are actually from my father?"

"Mmm-hmm." She nodded eagerly.

"And you think they're about your father sending scripts to mine?"

"That's right."

"But these letters don't talk about anything but rainy weather and buying a boat. What does that have to do with scripts?"

"It's in code, remember? Rainy weather concerns money, as in *Pennies from Heaven*."

Sean rolled his eyes.

She ignored him. "And when they wrote about buying a boat, they were describing how negotiations were going on a sale. It may seem a little obscure, but it's all in here."

"That's not obscure, it's opaque!" he retorted. "Not to mention silly. Why bother inventing this loony code in the first place?"

"Because of the blacklist. That's the reason my father wasn't still living in Toluca Lake and working for the studios. My father was paranoid about J. Edgar Hoover. The FBI didn't have very sophisticated surveillance methods in the fifties, but he was afraid they might figure out the post office box he used in Mexico and open his letters or packages. So he and your father used simple codes and wrote their letters in vague and misleading terms."

"No kidding." Sean was scanning one of the letters again. "You say this is a code, but this could mean nothing more than L.A. had a lot of rain in—" he turned the envelope over to look at the postmark "—in

1954, and somebody was buying a boat. As far as I can tell, that's all it says."

"Except that it's a code, and I've told you what the real meaning is."

"How long are you saying they kept this 007 stuff up?"

"Until your father died. Ten years ago."

"But that was *years* after the whole HUAC blacklist business had died away," Sean pointed out. "Didn't the blacklisted writers come home then and resume their careers?"

"Some did come home, a few, but not all of them were able to." She looked up at him, her eyes dark with sadness. "Some people managed to resume their careers after the blacklist was over, but many others never recovered what they'd lost. My father was one of those."

"What happened?"

"Nothing happened. No one offered him another job, no one asked him to write another script. He might as well have dropped off the face of the earth. As far as anyone in Hollywood was concerned, Philip Carruthers was as good as dead from the time the Committee subpoenaed him in 1951. The only person who didn't forget him was Whitey Baker, also known as Mo." She tapped the little notebook with her fingertip. "This notebook is the record of that."

Sean looked at her pitifully small stack of "proof" for several minutes, then shook his head.

"Hope, I've got to be honest with you. This notebook and the letters don't amount to proof. They're not even evidence. They don't appear to have anything to do with my father at all and could very well be nothing more than the fantasies and ramblings of a bitter, depressed old man who could very likely have suffered from senility and delusions.'' Hope bristled, but he went on. ''I have only your word that any of these cryptic remarks about rainy-day boat buying have anything to do with movie scripts.''

''And you don't believe me.'' She said it flatly, without emphasis or inflection.

''Would you, if you were in my position?'' he asked.

Hope bit her lip, looking down at the letters that were so precious to her, then up at him.

''I don't know,'' she admitted at last. ''It's all perfectly obvious to me, but then I've always known the truth. I've known about this all my life.''

''Well, I haven't. I never heard of any of this until you rang my doorbell this morning, and frankly, Miss Hope Carruthers, based on this little bit of evidence, I can't say I believe it.''

She watched his face for several seconds, then nodded, once.

''I see.'' She began gathering the papers and pushing them back into the envelope. ''In that case—'' she fastened the clasp with a twist that broke off one of the little brass ears ''—I won't take up any more of your time.'' She shoved herself out of her chair, clutching the precious envelope tightly. ''Goodbye, Mr. Boudreaux. It's been an . . . interesting evening.''

She turned on her heel and walked quickly away.

Chapter 3

Hope blinked back tears of disappointment and frustration as she hurried through the maze of tables and chairs, knowing she had to get out of there before the sense of bitter loss overwhelmed her tightly held control.

She'd honestly believed he would listen to her, and if he listened, she just knew she could make him believe her. She'd been so certain he would know about Whitey's part of the story. How could he not know? She'd been certain that Whitey Baker would have told his own son, if no one else, about the agreement with Philip.

But if Sean was telling her the truth, Whitey had said nothing to his son about the arrangement. And that simply didn't make sense to her. Hope found it difficult, no, impossible, to believe that the man's own son would know nothing of an arrangement this important, but either Sean Boudreaux honestly didn't know, or he was an extremely good actor, lying to her to protect his father's memory.

She didn't know the truth, but she was surprised by how badly she wanted Sean honestly not to know. It defied logic that Whitey's own son would be ignorant of his arrangement with Philip, but Hope wanted that to be true with an intensity that astonished her. She wanted him to be telling her the truth.

"Hope."

Sean caught up with her as she walked out the front door. She glanced over her shoulder, then bent her head, fishing in her purse for the parking chit.

"What do you want?"

"I'm not letting you go home like this."

"You can't stop me."

She handed the chit to the parking attendant and slipped a dollar in her pocket for the tip. She didn't know if a dollar was enough, but it was all she could spare.

"You're in no condition to drive." He took her elbow in a grip that was somewhere between imprisoning and proprietary.

"That's not for you to say." She jerked free of his grip as she heard the unmistakable clanking grumble of her car's engine.

"I'm going to see you home."

"How?" She tipped the valet with the grace of a duchess and let Sean hold the door while she slipped into the driver's seat. She gave him a smile of saccharine sweetness as she pushed the transmission lever into drive. "I think it's time for me to say good-night. Goodnight, Sean."

For all its rattles and rumbles, the old station wagon could move when she wanted it to. And tonight she wanted it to. She slid her foot from the brake to the accelerator and shot out of the restaurant's drive with a screech of tires. She was two blocks from the restaurant when she hit a stoplight and Sean caught up with her, darting through traffic to halt his low-slung black sports car just inches from her back bumper.

The light changed, and she moved off, and Sean moved off right behind her. Hope tried all the tricks as she threaded her way through the heavy Saturday-night traffic, sudden lane changes, quick turns, even a stretch on the freeway. She slipped her big car into spaces where it shouldn't have fit, dodged down an off ramp at the last minute and generally pushed the envelope of aggressive driving. Sean stuck with her all the way, a low-slung black shadow on her tail every time she looked in the rearview mirror.

When she finally parked at the curb in front of the attached bungalow she rented, he parked right behind her. She slid out, slammed the car door and marched quickly toward her front door, but Sean beat her to it, crossing the narrow strip of lawn in three strides.

"Do you always drive like that?" He plucked the keys from her hand and opened the door.

"Yes." Hope snatched back her keys and stalked through the doorway with Sean hot on her heels.

"It's a wonder you've survived this long." He caught her wrist and kept her beside him as they crossed the room. He switched on one lamp, then another. "Where'd you learn to drive, anyway?"

"Mexico City." She tried to pull free of his grip. "And will you *please* let go of me?"

"Not until I've checked the house for you," he said, "and I guess Mexico City explains the driving."

"You've been there?" She had no choice but to follow as he dragged her to the small kitchen.

"I've been there. The cab drivers terrify me." He turned on the kitchen light. "You're scarier than they are." He looked at the potted herbs on the windowsill and the Mexican copper pans hanging from a ceiling rack. "You've fixed this place up nice."

"Gee, thanks." She was pulled along as he checked her kitchen window, looked outside the back door and even inside the pantry. "I don't need you poking through my house, Sean!"

"I'm not poking. I'm checking to make sure no one broke in here while you were out. In a neighborhood like this, you can't be too careful."

"I'm quite careful enough, and this is a perfectly nice neighborhood!"

"Nice for muggers, maybe." He glanced into the bathroom, then stepped across the hall to Hope's bedroom. "And if you call that lock on your front door 'careful,' you're more naive than I thought. One of your second graders could open it with a credit card." He finally released her wrist to look inside her closet, swishing her few clothes aside and peering behind them.

"This is a nice neighborhood!" Hope retorted. "It may not be rich and fancy like yours, but I like it. And I won't have you talking about my students that way. They're good kids." She watched him close her closet door again, then turn to the bed. "What are you *doing?*"

He was crouching as she spoke, and she just stared as he bent to peer under the bed. When he sat back on his heels, she was standing in the doorway, arms folded, scowling.

"Well?" she asked. "Any psychotic ax murderers or desperate escaped convicts lurking under there?"

"Nothing but a couple of dust bunnies." He was grinning, but as he rose, the room, never large, suddenly seemed even smaller than usual. Hope skittered backward out of the doorway, retreating to the living room. Sean followed and found her standing by the front door in a clear invitation for him to take his leave.

"Gee, Hope—" he stopped in the middle of the room "—don't beat around the bush. If you want me to go, why not just say so?"

"Thank you for the dinner, Sean." She smiled, saccharine sweet. "Go home."

"Yes, ma'am. Whatever you say."

He walked across to her and reached up to prop one hand on the frame, trapping her between her chintz armchair and the iron-hard barrier of his arm.

Hope lifted her chin and scowled defiantly up at him. "It's late, Sean. Go home."

"I'm going, don't worry. There's just one more thing..."

"*Now* what?"

"Now this." He slid his free hand around the nape of her neck as he bent quickly to cover her mouth with his. It was a gentle kiss, seeking rather than demanding, and just as a little shiver of delight slid down Hope's spine, it ended.

She was swaying toward Sean, toward the strong, solid warmth of him, and her head was tipping back, more by instinct than design, when he lifted his lips from hers and stepped back.

He pulled the door open to leave, and Hope shivered in the flow of night air, cold without his warmth. He stepped out the door, then stopped and turned to look down at her.

"Good night, Hope Carruthers." He reached out to touch her cheek with a fingertip. "Sweet dreams."

He ran lightly across the grass to the street, and in moments, he and his black car had vanished into the night.

Hours later, Hope couldn't sleep.

She punched her pillow, flounced onto her back, jerked the sheet and blanket into place over her and tried to relax. It didn't work.

Sean Boudreaux had driven away from her house shortly before 11:00 p.m. At 2:26 in the morning, she was still wide-awake, her mind whirling with everything that had happened that day.

That day! She chuckled into the darkness. It was difficult to believe a single day could contain so much. Hope was left feeling as if several lifetimes had passed since she got up and made herself a cup of cinnamon-scented Mexican coffee that morning.

How could she persuade Sean Boudreaux that his father had really made an arrangement with Philip Carruthers 'way back in 1951, when Philip refused to answer that subpoena?

Why didn't Sean already know about the arrangement and the screenplays? He was Whitey's son, after all. Shouldn't he already know all this?

Or did he actually know? Was he aware of the arrangement and lying to her for reasons of his own? She frowned and rolled onto her side, bringing her knees up and hugging the pillow to her face. He'd as good as called her a liar when she told him what the letters and notebook meant. Was *he* lying to *her*?

Would he have kissed her if he was lying to her? Hope pressed her fingertips to her lips, where she fancied she could still feel Sean's kiss.

Why had he kissed her? For that matter, why had he wanted to dance with her at the restaurant?

She could still remember how she felt when he took her in his arms on that dance floor. Her stomach went all funny and her knees got weak; she felt light-headed and her heartbeat fluttered madly. And she'd always thought that stuff was just a convention of romantic novels!

Romantic novels or not, it was true. She'd felt hot and cold and shivery when he took her in his arms to dance, and even more when he'd kissed her. As a matter of fact, she felt kind of hot and cold and shivery just remembering.

This must have been what the other girls whispered and giggled about after lights-out in the dormitories. This was what they had felt when the boys from the academy had stolen kisses while the nuns' backs were turned.

Talk about delayed development! Hope laughed quietly into the darkness. What other girls felt with their first boyfriend at sixteen or seventeen, she was just experiencing for the first time at twenty-eight.

She hadn't received her first "real" kiss from an awkward boy of seventeen, though, but from an undeniably experienced man in his thirties. No wonder her head was spinning!

Chuckling softly, she rolled over, tucked the pillow beneath her head and slid into sleep.

"Hope? Are you all right?"

Hope blinked and refocused her gaze on the sun-baked playground, where her second-grade students were running off their after-lunch energy. She put two fingers to her lips and gave a piercing whistle.

"Tommy Chavez," she called, "put that rock down!" Tommy grimaced but did as he was told, replacing the pebble in a bed of stones around the base of a tall fan palm. Hope watched him run to join a group playing monkey in the middle, then turned to smile at the woman standing next to her.

Sister Margaret Lloyd, tall, thin and sixty-something, wore a businesslike dress, running shoes and the black-and-white veil of her order. She kept a hawklike eye on her sixth graders but glanced at Hope curiously, waiting for an answer.

"I'm okay, Margaret." Hope grinned at her friend. "I just have something on my mind."

"Tommy Chavez and his throwing arm?"

Hope shook her head. "It has to do with my family. There's a problem about my father's work."

"Is it anything I can help with?"

Hope shook her head, smiling to soften the refusal. Despite the gap in their ages, Margaret was more a friend than a mother figure. It was she who had smoothed the way for Hope to come from Mexico City, where she'd been teaching at one of the Order's schools, to Los Angeles, after Philip Carruthers died last year.

Hope wasn't sure what she'd have done without the Order, or friends like Margaret and the nuns in Mexico. They'd educated her, they'd given her a job so she could support her father in his last years of illness, they had helped her bury him, and then they had given her a way to come to America, to try to do what little she could to fulfill her father's long-denied dream.

Hope owed Margaret a great deal and could talk to her about almost anything, but this was a problem she would have to handle herself.

"Not this time, thank you, Margaret," she replied. "I'm not sure what to do about this, but I'll figure it out. I'll deal with it."

"I'm sure you will. I've always found that problems are best faced head-on, if that's of any assistance," Margaret told her. She glanced at the plain man's watch on her wrist. "Time's up." She blew three blasts on the coach's whistle she wore on a cord around her neck. "Back to the salt mines."

"Back to my science lesson." Hope grinned as the teachers scattered around the playground began assembling their classes to go inside.

"What are you working on?" Margaret asked.

"Growing plants. And thank goodness the bean seeds we planted last week sprouted! I don't know what I'd have done about my lesson plan if they hadn't!"

"You'd deal with it, just like you always do. Just as you'll deal with this problem of yours."

"Head-on, right?" Hope grinned again and went to collect her class.

That thought lay in the back of her mind as she and the children talked about how and why the bean seeds had sprouted, reviewed subtraction and read a story. By the time Hope left school, she'd come to a decision.

She would take Margaret's advice and face her problem, namely Sean Boudreaux, head-on.

Within an hour of leaving work, she'd hurried home to wash her face and brush her hair, and she was headed up the canyon toward his house again. She hadn't phoned Sean, a deliberate omission, and there was no one in sight when she pulled to a stop in front of his house.

She pressed the doorbell and listened to Big Ben's chimes reverberating in the distance again, and in a few minutes a scowling Sean pulled the door open. His expression changed to puzzlement when he saw Hope.

"What are you doing here?" he asked, then shook his head. "I apologize. That was rude. Hello. And what are you doing here?"

"Hello." She smiled, a little uncertainly. "I'm here because I need to talk to you."

"I thought we did that last night."

"Yes." She looked down, then up at him again. "But we didn't settle anything."

"What's to settle?"

"What we're going to do," she replied. "What else?"

"What do you mean what else? We're not going to do anything, because there isn't anything to do."

"Of course there is! We have to find out the truth!"

"We already know the truth," he said flatly. "My father was a producer and screenwriter, and your father went to Mexico during the blacklist. That's all there is to it."

"You know that isn't all there is to it." Hope stepped forward. "May I come in?"

He studied her for a moment. "You're not going anywhere until we have this conversation, are you?"

"No."

He stepped back, swinging the door wide. "Come on in."

Hope decided to overlook his less than gracious tone. He'd allowed her in and he was going to talk to her. She couldn't really ask for more than that.

Sean wouldn't talk about anything until they were settled in the airy living room with coffee and mineral water set out on the low table in front of the sofa.

"All right." He sat back, watching her over the rim of his coffee cup, his face expressionless. "What is it you want?"

"I want to find the proof of my father's arrangement with your father."

"Assuming there is any of this so-called 'proof.'"

"There is." The conviction in her voice was a sharp contrast to the slightly sarcastic skepticism in his.

"Sure." He sipped his coffee. "So, how do you propose to find this phantom proof?"

This was the moment Hope had waited for with both anticipation and dread. "Sean," she asked, "have you looked through your father's papers?"

"A few of them. I had to find the bank books and deeds and things like that when the estate was probated."

"Have you looked through his records of the movie business? Not the financial things, but the records of scripts he sold or produced, things he accepted and rejected, the records of the creative side of his business?"

Sean shook his head.

"That's where the records of his arrangement with my father must be, then."

"If they even exist."

"They do exist. What I'd like to do is search your father's records to find them."

For a moment Sean was silent and still. Then, slowly and carefully, he set his cup on the tray. "You want to *what?*"

"Search his records for the proof," she repeated.

"Just like that? You show up on my doorstep insisting that my father didn't write the movies that the whole world knows he wrote and announce that you want to look through his papers? Those are papers I haven't even seen yet, and I'm researching his biography!" Sean shoved himself up off the sofa and walked a couple of paces away before wheeling around to glare at her. "Lady, you have one hell of a nerve!"

Hope ignored that. "Are you going to talk about the movies he produced in his biography?"

"And the movies he wrote," Sean replied. "Of course I am. They were the real love of his life. He made far more money from real estate than from movies, but the production company was his heart and soul."

"So you're going to write about it. Do you want to tell the truth?"

"Certainly. He was my father, but that doesn't mean I was blind to his faults." Sean's eyes darkened and he looked away. "If anything, I knew his faults better than most. Yes," he said to Hope, "I'm going to tell the truth."

"Then don't you think you should make sure you know the whole truth?" she suggested, almost gently.

Sean turned back to her. "I want to know the truth," he admitted after a moment.

"And if there was something you didn't know about your own father, something this important, you would want to know it, wouldn't you?"

"If there was something this important, don't you think I'd already—" Sean stopped. His mouth twisted in a small, bitter smile. "No, I might not already know. For most of my life I never really knew my own father at all."

"Do you want to?" Hope asked.

There was a long silence before Sean spoke. "I don't know that I really want to know everything Whitey was capable of. . . but I think I have to. If I'm ever going to have any kind of peace, I have to."

"Then let me search the records for you," she pleaded. "If you're going to write his biography, you'll have to go through his papers anyway, won't you?"

"Yeah, eventually I will."

"I can help you. I can go through his papers for you, even put them in order if you like."

"While you're looking for some record of this 'deal' between your father and mine?"

"That's right."

"But there *aren't* any records! Can't you see that this whole business is crazy?"

"No, I can't, because it's not crazy, it's true! And since it's true, Sean, your father *must* have kept some kind of records. They might be in code, like my father's, or they might be in plain English. They might be out in plain sight or they might be hidden in among his other papers."

"Hidden in plain sight."

"What?" she wondered, then nodded. "That's right. But they must be there somewhere."

"And why must they?"

"Because this was a complicated business. It went on for almost thirty years. He'd have *had* to keep records."

Sean looked down, then up again at her. "You're not going to give this up, are you?"

Hope shook her head, her hair swinging around her shoulders. Her eyes were limpid and clear and bottomless as an emerald sea. Siren's eyes, Sean thought, his writer's mind automatically supplying the metaphor. Siren's eyes and an innocent heart.

And an obsession. He could read the depth of her obsession in those siren's eyes, in the passion in her voice when she spoke about it. No, she wasn't going to give up, and this was no child's quest. She might be a little naive, a little unworldly, but she wasn't a child. She was a woman, with a woman's tenacity, a woman's determination.

There was something intriguing about the blending of naiveté and passion. It was too bad she was destined to be disappointed in this quixotic quest of hers.

It was too bad she didn't realize she was driving him crazy in ways he was pretty sure she was too innocent to be aware of. He didn't know how well Hope had slept after that kiss last night, but he hadn't rested easily.

She was a problem he didn't need, a complication that would be far better avoided, and all he wanted was to kiss her again. Kiss her, and hold her, and make love to her long into the night.... Sean made sure his thoughts didn't show in his face. If sheltered, convent-schooled Hope knew what big bad Sean was thinking, she'd run for her life.

She wasn't running, though. She was watching him with those huge emerald eyes in that cameo face, begging him to let her involve herself in his life.

"Do you have any idea what you're asking?" he said abruptly.

"All I want to do is to look through his papers."

"It'll take weeks. Maybe months."

"Don't be silly. I went through my father's papers in a few days. It won't take me long."

"How many papers did your father have?"

"Three whole file cabinets," she told him. "Plus some boxes."

"That's it?" He laughed, incredulous. "That's nothing."

"They were big boxes!"

"Three measly file cabinets and a few boxes?" Sean scoffed. "That's trivial. You want to see what my father left?" He reached for her hand. "Come on."

Sean had chosen to use the solarium at the west end of the house as his office. Whitey's study, at the rear of the house, looking out at the pool, was as he'd left it ten years before. Sean led Hope down the hall and stopped outside the door.

"You sure you want to see what my father left behind?"

"I said I did." Hope frowned, confused. "Why are you making such a big thing of this, Sean? It's only some papers, after all."

"Only?" Sean laughed. "Take a look."

He swung the door open, flicked on the lights and stood back.

"Oh...my..." Hope walked slowly into the room, staring around her in disbelief.

"Oh, my," Sean repeated. "Yeah, that about covers it, although what I said the first time I saw this room was a little more...blunt."

"What *is* all this?"

Hope gaped in shock at stacks of boxes overflowing with papers, at ranks of file drawers from floor to ceiling, at shelves crammed with books and scripts and fat file folders spilling their contents onto the chaos. The desk was even worse. Looking a little more closely, she could just about tell that beneath the avalanche of paper was a massive mahogany antique. There were even folded sheets stuck in the curlicues of a filigreed brass desk lamp.

"This," Sean told her dryly, "is what Whitey Baker left for posterity."

"But you're going to write his biography. Haven't you sorted his papers?"

"Does it look like I've sorted them? I dug out the stuff the lawyers needed when the estate was probated, but that was all. I could make a full-time job of sorting through all this, but I already have a full-time occupation, and I still have to make a living. Yeah, I'm researching the biography, but I haven't gotten very far into it. I dig around in here when I need something specific, but that's all the sorting I can manage right now."

He looked at the chaos in the room, then at Hope, who had picked her way across to the overflowing desk.

"Want to give up?"

She straightened and looked back at him. "No. No, I don't. I have to find the proof of my father's work, and I know it must be somewhere in here."

"It's going to be worse than looking for a needle in a haystack, you know."

"I don't care. I want to do it. And it will help you, too, you know," she added eagerly. "I can't search methodically unless I sort this and organize it as I go along. Then it'll be much easier for you to use. Will you let me?"

"It'd be like giving someone permission to dig a swimming pool with a teaspoon."

"I don't mind."

"Maybe I do mind." Sean leaned back against the door frame and folded his arms across his chest, watching her. His face was in shadow, and Hope couldn't read his expression. "I don't know anything about you. You waltz in here with a story that nobody in their right mind would believe and want me to let you go through my father's private papers? Why should I?''

"Because it's right," Hope told him softly. "You and I are strangers, but our fathers were true friends, closer than brothers. I'm asking you to let me do this in the name of their friendship."

Sean didn't speak but looked past her at the chaotic room. "If I let you do this, *before* I let you do this, I want you to tell me the whole story. Everything you know about your father and mine, about this deal of theirs, about you and your life in Mexico with your father. Everything."

"All right." Hope would have agreed to more than that for this opportunity. Sean studied the room for several minutes more, and Hope held her breath while she waited for him to decide. It was very quiet. She could hear the traffic swishing by on the canyon road and the raucous cry of a scrub jay from the hillside above the house. Her breathing sounded loud in the silence, and her palms grew damp.

"Damned if I know why," Sean said at last, "but yes, I'll let you do it."

Hope picked her way back across the room and stopped in front of him. She regarded him gravely for several moments, then a smile spread across her face, curving her lips and warming her eyes. It was like the sun breaking through morning fog, warming Sean in the glow.

"Thank you," she said softly, and rose on tiptoe to kiss his cheek.

Hours after she had gone home, Sean could still feel that butterfly's brush of a kiss on his skin.

Chapter 4

"So they went to Mexico."

"That's right."

"And you said he kept writing, but what did you do?"

"I wasn't born yet."

"Oh. Well, once you were, born that is, what was it like for you, growing up there? Where did you go to school?"

"I told you. Our Lady of Guadalupe boarding school."

"Oh, yeah, the nuns. Grade school and high school both, right?"

He looked down at the notes he'd been making, and checked something off. Probably checking to see that she wasn't changing her answers, Hope thought.

"Yes," she replied, as patiently as she could. "And college, too."

Sean leaned an elbow on the table and sipped his coffee. "What did you do after college?"

"I went to work. My father was elderly, and he wasn't well."

"So you got a job as a teacher?"

"Yes. That's how I was able to come to L.A., as a matter of fact. I taught at one of the Order's schools in Mexico City, and after my father died, when I told them I wanted to come to America, they arranged for me to come here and teach at St. Bartholomew's."

"That was convenient."

"It was more than that," she told him. "It made the impossible possible. I have a lot to be grateful to the Sisters for."

"Mmm-hmm." He thought for a moment about all she'd told him, then looked up into her eyes. He was not smiling as he asked, "Why did you want to come to America?"

Hope frowned. "Why?"

"That's right, why? You said you told the Sisters you wanted to come to America, and they helped you, but you didn't say why you wanted to come."

"I would think that's obvious. I'm American. I wanted to come home."

"But you were born in Mexico and lived there all your life. I would think that Mexico was home."

Hope shook her head, smiling gently. "We were an Anglo family. I was never anything but the foreigner, the *norteamericana*. I had American citizenship from my parents, an American passport. The only thing I didn't have was an American address."

"So you came home to a home you'd never known," he said. "What was it like?"

"You mean, what *is* it like?" She smiled. "I haven't even been here a year yet. And it's strange. Surreal. It's both familiar and unfamiliar, comforting and frightening at the same time. So many things seem so familiar, yet I hardly know anyone outside the teachers and students at school and their families. I've come home, but I'm still a stranger."

"So that's why you came back. Because this is home."

"And because it was my father's home. And because I wanted to honor his name by arranging for him to get credit for the movies he wrote."

"Which brings us back to square one, doesn't it?" Sean said. "You say your father wrote movies that the whole world is sure my father wrote, and I think my father wrote them, and who knows which of us is right?"

"I know."

Sean gave her a speaking look. "Don't start that with me again, okay? Let's just leave it that nobody knows anything for sure until we've got some concrete proof."

"All right," Hope agreed after a moment. "We'll find the proof first."

Whitey's old study was a large room, but Hope felt crowded in there. It wasn't the accumulated chaos of years of occupation by a man with a pack-rat mentality that left her feeling claustrophobic, and it wasn't the heaps and piles of papers everywhere. It was Sean.

Hope took another folder from the box on the desk beside her, blew the dust off and opened it. She scanned the first letter in what appeared to be a stack of them, then glanced up from beneath her lashes.

Sean was scowling at his laptop computer, one hand shoved into his hair as he tapped a key at intervals, reading what he'd written. From his attitude, he might not even have been aware she was there, but Hope knew better. She never seemed to catch him looking at her, but she could feel his eyes on her when she had her back turned or when she was bent over her papers.

She could feel his suspicion like a tangible thing, and she knew what he was watching for. He wanted to make sure she didn't slip some fabricated evidence of her own into Whitey's papers. The fact that she would never consider doing something so dishonest cut no ice with Sean. He made it clear he didn't trust her out of his sight for a moment.

And that hurt.

The very first day, after she'd told him all she could about her father, her family, her childhood in Mexico, he'd brought her to the study to work on the papers. She'd been surprised to see that he'd cleared off a dusty Chippendale console on the far side of the room, beside the windows, and equipped it as a desk, with a Tiffany lamp on top and a Queen Anne side chair behind it.

It wasn't for her, he'd informed her curtly when she thanked him for clearing a work area. It was for him. While she was sorting the papers, he'd bring his portable computer in and work in this room. Hope had been about to ask why, when she realized. It was obvious, painfully so.

"I see," was all she'd said, but the hurt went deep. She'd never had anyone suspect her of dishonesty before, never had anyone distrust her so obviously.

And thus it had gone, every afternoon since the first. When Hope arrived, Sean brought his laptop to Whitey's study, and while she sorted at the massive mahogany desk, in the center of the room, he sat at his improvised desk by the windows, alternately clicking rapidly on the keys and staring into space, lost in what she imagined was deeply creative thought, all the while making sure she didn't fabricate any of the evidence she was searching for.

It hurt, and it made her angry, and of the two, anger was more easily borne. Of course, she thought in righteous irritation, how was she to know that she could trust Sean? She could tell that he didn't want her to find the proof she so desperately sought. How was she to know he wouldn't destroy whatever turned up, so he could continue to deny the arrangement between their fathers?

He raked a hand impatiently through his hair, and one ebony lock flopped forward onto his brow as he bent over the computer and began typing rapidly. Hope might not trust Sean any more than he trusted her, but as she watched him, her fingers itched to push that lock of hair back to see if it was as soft as it looked. She curled her hand into a fist to suppress the urge. The way Sean felt about her, he'd hardly welcome that kind of familiarity.

"Hope?"

"What?" She blinked, startled out of her reverie.

"Is something wrong?"

"N-no. What would be wrong?"

"I'm asking you. You were sitting there staring into space and frowning. What were you thinking about?"

She blushed, all too aware of what he'd say if he knew what she was thinking. "Nothing, really. My mind was just wandering, I guess."

"Something interesting in that folder?"

"Not really." She lifted a couple of pages, then let them drop. "It just looks like more correspondence with the studio's accounting department."

Sean grinned wryly. "Whitey at his sarcastic best, I suppose."

Hope had to smile in return. "He didn't have a lot of patience with the cautious, bottom-line types, did he?"

"Not much. It may make you feel better to know they were well paid to put up with his tirades, though. He was volatile, but he was fair to the people who worked for him."

"That's nice to know. I've noticed, though, that the comptroller and the studio's chief of accounting gave as good as they got."

"Yeah. Whitey might have played the tyrant, but he admired anybody who'd stand up to him. The studio execs knew that, of course. It made for some exciting meetings."

"I can imagine."

"Yeah," Sean replied absently. "Well, I've got to get this done." His eyes were back on the screen as he spoke.

Hope knew a rebuff when it smacked her in the face. Sean didn't want to talk to her, didn't want to share a smile and Whitey's foibles with her. He wanted, in fact, as little to do with her as possible, and it was only the fact that he distrusted her that kept him in the same room with her. Biting her lip against the sting of embarrassment, she bent over Whitey's letters again.

Sean typed rapidly for a few minutes, then stopped, looked at the screen and swore silently. Gibberish. He sat in this room with Hope each evening and wrote gibberish. He couldn't concentrate on anything when she was in the room, certainly not on this article on nuclear physics that he'd promised his agent would be done soon.

In fact, the only thing he seemed to be able to concentrate on was Hope Carruthers herself.

And Lord knew he'd tried to concentrate on just about anything else.

It wasn't as if she were worldly or sophisticated or theatrically talented. He knew women who were worldly and sophisticated, women with awesome talent. He forgot them moments after they said goodbye, but he couldn't get convent-schooled second-grade teacher Hope Carruthers out of his mind.

He glanced at her from beneath half-closed lids. She was studying the papers in front of her, her lower lip pushed out in a little pout of concentration, thick dark lashes hiding her emerald eyes. She didn't have that surface glitter, but she was beautiful in an ethereal, almost otherworldly kind of way. With her fair skin and soft dark hair and softly feminine clothes, she was an anachronism in the fast-paced, high-fashion world of Los Angeles. She wasn't flashy or theatrical, but she seemed to glow from within, with a luminous beauty that didn't need flash or glitter.

Maybe it was her lips that got to him, soft and pink and naked of paint. It had been an impulse to kiss her, one he should have resisted, for now he knew that she tasted of springtime, not cosmetics, that beneath her innocence and inexperience were a quiet maturity and a surprising passion. Or perhaps it was her eyes that got to him. He'd never seen eyes quite that color, full of hidden depths and secret fire. Maybe it was her eyes, or maybe it was the combination of passion and innocence that haunted him, but haunt him she did.

He waited for her arrival around four-thirty each afternoon with a mixture of anticipation and dread, eager to see her, dreading the tense two hours they would spend working in Whitey's study. He knew she didn't trust him, that she suspected if she actually found any evidence of this "arrangement" between Whitey and her father, he would just as soon get rid of it and pretend it never existed.

That wasn't true. He wasn't the type to lie. But Sean didn't bother telling Hope that. She wouldn't believe him, anyway. She'd cast him as the villain of this piece, and he didn't see any way to change her mind. On the other hand, how could he be sure she wouldn't slip some bit of so-called evidence into the papers she was sorting, just so she could say that Whitey actually had had some weird kind of deal with her father? Convent school or not, how did he know he could trust this lady with the innocent lips and passionate eyes?

Each afternoon passed like the others, the two of them working on their respective sides of the room. They worked in silence for the most part, until, at six-thirty, Hope straightened the papers she was working on, picked up her purse, said good-evening and left. Sean didn't know what she did in the evenings; he'd never asked. He could imagine it, though, Hope going home to her little apartment, fixing herself a meal, reading or correcting papers until she went to bed.

His own evenings seemed to follow a pattern, too. He ate, either the meal the housekeeper left in the refrigerator two or three times a week or carryout from one of the little ethnic places at the bottom of the canyon road. His personal favorites were antipasto salad from Ristorante Napolitano and noodles with peanut sauce from the Bangkok House. The Thai leftovers weren't bad for breakfast, either, if you didn't mind hot chilies. He didn't.

On that particular evening, Sean watched Hope's old dinosaur of a station wagon grumble its way down the drive, then went to see if he had any noodles left from yesterday. He didn't even bother to toss them in the microwave but carried the carton, a pair of chopsticks and a can of beer out to the patio, where he settled into a lounger under the pergola to eat his noodles cold.

Dusk was closing in rapidly, but a late-feeding hummingbird swooped down and hovered eighteen inches in front of Sean's face. The tiny jewel-colored bird studied him for several seconds, then returned to the nectar feeder hanging from the pergola.

The telephone's ring shattered the quiet evening, jangling Sean out of his reverie and sending the hummingbird swooping away over the trees by the patio in search of a quieter dinner. Sean watched him go, then switched on the cordless phone he'd brought out.

"Hello?"

"Hi, stranger," said Sean's literary agent, a smile in his voice.

"Don, how are you?" Sean propped the phone on his shoulder and fished some more noodles out of the carton. "What's up?"

"I was about to ask you that," replied Don Molinari. "How's the book coming?"

"Don't you mean the article on nuclear physics for the layman? It's coming along."

"Is it coming fast enough to make your deadline? They want that on Monday, you know."

"I'll make it. I'll messenger it over to you on Sunday night."

"Great. The editor will be glad to hear it. How about your father's biography? Are things going well on that?"

"Well..." Sean sighed heavily. "The preliminary research is...going."

"I don't like the sound of that. What's wrong?"

"It's not that anything's wrong. I've just run into kind of a snag."

"Define 'kind of a snag.'"

"Nothing disastrous. Some new allegations about my father's work have come to my attention, and I need to check them out, that's all."

"What allegations? You hit all the high points when you roughed out an outline for the publishers, didn't you? What else have you found out?"

"I haven't found out anything for sure, Don. It's just some allegations. I'm working with a source to clear up the confusion."

"What confusion?" Don demanded. "Sean, can you just tell me what this is all about?"

"No." Sean's refusal was quiet but firm. "There's nothing to say until I check it out, Don. If you need to know, I'll tell you."

"I can't tell you what great comfort it is to know that."

"You can handle it, Don. You're tough. How's Susie?"

"Susie's great. The baby is, too. We saw his picture on the ultrasound last week."

The deliberate distraction worked like a charm, just as Sean had known it would. After thirty-six years of bachelorhood, Don had been blissfully married to Susie just about six months. From being a confirmed bachelor, he'd become the staunchest, and most vocal, of advocates for the institution of marriage. Now that Susie was expecting their first child, his cup of enthusiasm was running over. All Sean had to do was mention Susie or the expected child, and Don was off and running.

"They really can tell it's a boy," Don was replying to Sean's skeptical question. "And don't think I don't know you changed the subject. I'll let you get away with it for now, but we will get back to this business of new allegations about your father."

"If there's anything you need to know, Don, I'll be sure to tell you."

"You're all heart."

"I know."

Sean switched off the phone, smiling. Don was more than just an agent, he was a good friend. Sean would tell him whatever Don needed to know, when and if the time came.

He leaned back in the lounger again and fished around in the bottom of the carton for the last bite of noodles. Dusk had become night while he and Don were talking. In the distance a coyote yipped and was answered by hysterical barking from a dog somewhere farther up the canyon. The hummingbird hadn't returned but had gone to wherever hummingbirds go at night.

Allegations had come to his attention, he'd told Don. Allegations. If, in the most unlikely scenario he could imagine, even a fraction of those allegations should prove to be true, the story of Whitey Baker's "secret life" would stand the Hollywood community on its ear.

Did Hope know that? Did she care?

Where was Hope tonight? Sean wondered. What were her thoughts?

* * *

Where was Hope?

Sean watched a big brown UPS truck lumber past his driveway, then stalked back to his desk and dropped into the chair. He looked at the words glowing on the computer screen, but they made no sense.

That was nothing new. He hadn't written a sensible word since four that afternoon, when, as usual, he started watching for Hope's arrival.

She should have arrived punctually at four-thirty, just as she did every day. She hadn't mentioned any after-school meetings or appointments, hadn't told him she'd be late, but four-thirty had come and gone, and then five, and five-fifteen, and Hope hadn't arrived.

Where was she?

He glanced at his watch. It was now five twenty-five, and she was nearly an hour late.

Sean had reached the point of leaping out of his chair to stare out the window every time he heard a motor vehicle outside. Adolescent behavior, he knew, but Hope was late, and Sean was beyond doing anything about his behavior.

Where was she?

With quick, impatient taps he shut the computer down, returning to the window twice during the process. There was no point in pretending to work; he might as well just sit by the window and watch for Hope. "And fret and worry, too," he muttered to himself. It didn't seem to matter that he knew he was acting stupid. He couldn't help himself.

Hope Carruthers might be a thorn in his side and a pain in his neck, but he couldn't help worrying about her. She was too trusting of people, too certain of the goodness inside them. In a city like L.A. it didn't pay to be too trusting, for there were a lot of people out there just waiting to take advantage of that trust. Had someone taken advantage of her trust?

And her driving! He'd offered to pay for a cab to his house each evening, and she'd turned him down with a laugh. She liked driving, and she didn't especially like cabs. So each evening she drove to his house through rush-hour traffic. He didn't like to think of her flinging that antique monster of a car through traffic with her usual pedal-to-the-metal driving style. It was nothing more than a disaster waiting to happen. Maybe it had already happened.

Where *was* Hope, anyway?

He yanked the curtains aside, glared out at the road, then dropped the curtains and stalked out of the room. Wherever she was, she was late, so something was wrong, and he was going to find her.

He stuck a note for her on the front door in case he missed her and she arrived at the house before he got back, then started down the canyon.

He drove slowly, ignoring the line of cars piling up behind him, trying to watch oncoming traffic while scanning the sides of the winding road for signs that anyone had gone over. He reached the intersection at the bottom of the canyon without seeing Hope's station wagon, either on the road or off it. That didn't notably ease his worry, because he still didn't know where the hell she was!

And which streets had she said she took to his house each day? He couldn't remember them all, though he'd asked her once, out of the same curiosity that prompted anyone who dealt with L.A. traffic to inquire about preferred freeway routes and secrets to avoiding the worst of the rush-hour nightmares.

Well, Sean had asked, but now that he needed to, he couldn't remember if she'd said Sunset or Santa Monica, the Hollywood Freeway or the San Diego. And because he couldn't remember, he drove them all, up one, down another, burning with frustration as he crept along in the overwhelming crush of evening traffic.

He drove for an agonizing hour before he found her, and then he was so anxious to make it through the intersection of Santa Monica and Beverly after sitting through three lights that he almost missed her. At the last possible moment, he saw her car in the middle of a multicar rear-end collision. He saw her car, but he didn't see Hope.

Swearing viciously, Sean swung across two lanes of traffic, ignoring blaring horns and shouted imprecations, to reach the knot of onlookers and police standing by the disabled cars. Heedless of both police and looky-loos, he shoved his way into the crowd.

"Hope! My God, Hope, are you all right?"

Shoving past the policeman she was talking to, Sean grabbed her shoulder and swung her around, into his arms. He crushed her to him, burying his face in her hair, eyes shut tight against the surge of emotion that threatened to overwhelm him. He held her like that until the tightness in his throat began to loosen, then lifted his head and eased his hold on her just enough to look her over.

"Are you all right?" he demanded. "Are you hurt anywhere?" He ran his hands down her arms and back, tilted her head to look into her face. "Are you okay?" She seemed to be, so he dragged her back into his arms again. "What the hell happened, anyway?"

"I'm fine," Hope replied, muffled against his shoulder, "but I'd be better if you'd let me breathe."

"Oh." Sean couldn't have cared less that they were in the middle of a crowd of people, including police, but he didn't want to keep Hope from breathing. He straightened and stepped back a bit, but kept his arm around Hope's waist.

"Yeah. Sorry." He looked down at Hope once more. "Are you sure you're okay?"

She stood very straight and stiff within his arm, not pulling away but far from relaxed. Her voice when she spoke was high and breathless, and Sean felt a pang of remorse. He'd been overwhelmed with relief, but that didn't mean he had to squash her.

"I'm fine," she reassured him. "My car's not, but I am."

"And while we're on the subject—" the policeman had been waiting patiently for the reunion to be completed, but he broke in when he saw his chance "—could I get the rest of your statement, Ms. Carruthers?" He glanced at Sean, still with his arm firmly around Hope's waist. "I take it you're a...friend?" he said dryly.

"That's right." Sean's cold, level regard dared the officer to make something of that. "And I'd like to know what happened here?"

The cop regarded him coolly for a moment, then nodded. "It appears that Ms. Carruthers's car was approaching the intersection when the light changed to red. She, with two cars in front of her, stopped for the light, but the car behind her, a—" he consulted his notepad, then glanced at the tangle the tow trucks were in the process of disentangling "—a black late-model Mercedes sedan, apparently failed to see the light, didn't slow down in time and hit Ms. Carruthers's car, pushing it into the two cars in front. Is that right, Ms. Carruthers?''

"Yes. I looked in my mirror as I was stopping, and all I could see was this black car coming at me, so fast..." Her voice wobbled and she stopped, swallowing hard.

Sean bent to look into her face. "You're sure you're okay?"

She nodded. "I'm okay. It's just that it all happened so fast. And my car—"

Sean followed her gaze to the station wagon, hooked up to a tow truck. The back end was crumpled in, shortened by almost a foot, lights shattered and bumper dangling drunkenly, while the front end, where she'd been pushed into the car in front of her, looked almost as bad. Those lights were shattered, too, the hood buckled up, and blue coolant was dripping slowly from her cracked radiator. The damage probably wasn't terminal, but her crunched car looked sadly forlorn, trundling away on the tow truck's hook.

"They'll take care of your car, ma'am." The officer fished a card from his pocket. "You can call this number after eight tomorrow morning to tell them where you're having your car taken for repairs, all right?"

"Okay." She tucked the card into her purse.

"Here's your registration and insurance card." She took those, too. "Your insurance agent can help with the rest of the details. Can you take her home, sir?"

"Yes. I'll take care of her." Sean led her away from the accident site as the officer left them to finish up with another of the victims.

"Sean?" Hope stopped short in the middle of the sidewalk, pulling free of his arm.

"What? What's wrong?"

"My car! What do I do about it?"

"You call the number on that card tomorrow and tell them which body shop will be picking your car up. Come on." He led her a few steps farther, then she stopped again.

"But how do I know what body shop to choose? I don't know anything about body shops."

"I know a place you can call. Now, come *on*." He pulled her along once more.

"But I've got to call the insurance man—"

"I have phones at my house. If you can't wait that long, I have a phone in the car. Just come on!"

She went. She didn't go happily, but she went.

She did call her insurance agent from the car, and though Sean rolled his eyes at her anxious impatience, she called the garage, too, giving them the information the policeman had given her and receiving their assurances that they'd give her trusty wagon the best of care.

"Are you happy now?" Sean didn't bother to hide the sarcasm. They were both tense with the delayed effects of worry and fear, and her concern for that clunker of a car was beginning to irritate the hell out of him. She needed to worry about herself, not that damned car.

"No." Hope glanced at him, then turned to look out the window again. "I'll be happy when my car's fixed."

"Always assuming they can fix it." Sean swung into his driveway and downshifted. The powerful engine snarled as he started uphill. "Always assuming they can find parts that old."

"Gee, thanks!" Hope flung open her door as soon as he stopped. "How nice of you to be encouraging." She tossed the words over her shoulder as she slid out of the car and stalked toward the front door. "It's *so* tactful, and just what I need to hear tonight!"

Sean slammed his own door and followed on her heels.

"If you want warm fuzzies, Hope, watch *Sesame Street* on TV. I'm telling you the truth."

"You're being negative because you don't like my car."

"I'm being realistic, because I know that no car lasts forever, and that one's been running on borrowed time for years."

Hope jerked to a halt in the middle of the entry hall and rounded on Sean. "Stop that, Sean! It's not funny! Just because I'm not rich like you and I can't afford a brand-new fancy car every year, that's no reason to make fun of me!"

"Who's making fun? I'm not laughing. All I'm doing is telling you today what the body shop guys are going to tell you tomorrow." He passed her, heading for the kitchen. "I'm doing you a favor, if you want to know the truth. And I'm not the one who's rich. My father was rich."

"I know." Hope followed him to the kitchen, where he was noisily ransacking his cupboards for dishes and cutlery. "He made several fortunes, and he was smart and generous and a good friend, and he sold my father's screenplays for him."

"And you're going to find some kind of proof of this supposed arrangement in my father's papers," Sean recited, singsong, "and we're right back where I came into this farce." He rummaged in the refrigerator, setting an assortment of containers out on the counter.

"It is not a farce! And you have *no* business saying—"

"Lady, I can say whatever I want!" Sean slammed the refrigerator door and whirled on her, his dark eyes flashing with fury.

"I can say what I damned well please! You're the one who turned up at my door, spinning a tale that, frankly, only an idiot would believe! But on the strength of what even you must realize is a perfectly preposterous story, I've let you come into my house, I've let you go through my father's papers, through things even I haven't seen, knowing all the time that if you can find any kind of so-called proof of this loony story of yours, you'll use it to destroy my father's reputation!"

Hope was staring at him, her mouth open in shock. "Is *that* what you think?"

"What else is there to think?" He set one last carton on the counter and slammed the refrigerator door.

"You could think that maybe I'm right!" Hope followed as Sean carried an armload of carryout food cartons across the kitchen to the microwave. "You could think that maybe I'm right about the arrangement between your father and mine! Or maybe you already know that, don't you?"

Sean stuffed several cartons in the microwave and punched buttons to start it cooking. "What the hell are you talking about?"

"That's pretty much what you said when I first told you about this, but how do I know it's true?" she demanded. "How do I know you didn't know all about the arrangement between our fathers before I showed up? You've accused me of planning to destroy your father's reputation, but how do I know what lengths you'd go to to *protect* his reputation?"

"What are you saying?" Sean turned to look at her, his eyes cold. Behind him, the microwave dinged. He ignored it. "If there's something you want to say, Hope, don't beat around the bush, just say it."

"All right. I'll say it." Hope lifted her chin, refusing to be cowed by his anger. "You say my story is preposterous? It's no more preposterous than your expecting me to believe that Whitey Baker's own son never knew about something as important as this. Maybe you did know about it, and maybe you don't want the world to know."

"And maybe," Sean said slowly, "you've talked your way into my home not to find evidence but to plant it. Maybe you're planning to slip something into my father's papers and prove something that never happened!"

"How dare—"

Sean caught her wrist on the upswing before the slap connected with his face. He forced her arm back down again.

"Don't do anything you'll be sorry for, Hope. Don't even think about it."

Hope jerked hard against his grip, but Sean held her with insulting ease.

"Maybe I've already done something dumb." She glared up at Sean. "Maybe I was dumb to trust you. You accuse me of planning to plant fake evidence, but what about you?"

"What about me?"

Hope stopped trying to pull away from his steel grip on her wrist and took a half step closer, her face tight with a fury to match Sean's.

"How do I know," she asked softly, "that you aren't in there every afternoon watching me, waiting for me to find evidence so you can get rid of it and preserve your father's precious reputation?"

Chapter 5

Sean looked down at her, his lips twisting in anger. His grip on her wrist tightened, and he drew her inexorably closer until she had to tip her head back to look at him, until a scant inch separated them.

"I ought—" The words were low, rough with the effort he was exerting to control his anger.

"I ought to slap you!" Hope retorted.

Infuriatingly, Sean laughed. "You already tried that. It didn't work, did it?"

"You deserve it!"

"No more than you, little Hope." His voice was still quiet, but there was cold anger beneath the almost gentle words.

"So you're going to slap me?" she said, her voice higher and thinner than it should have been.

"No." He shook his head, shifting his grip from her wrists to her upper arms. "Not a slap. Never..." He moved too quickly for her to guess what he meant to do, much less evade his lips as he captured her mouth.

For a moment, only a moment, the pressure of his mouth was hard, almost punishing, but the angry kiss didn't last, couldn't last, for the tension that seemed to live between them like a separate presence became a kind of magic when they touched.

Sean's lips gentled, moving on hers, asking a question that her own softening lips and newly pliant body answered. His grip on her arms loosened, even as she clutched at his sleeves, rising onto her toes, reaching for his kiss.

Sean shifted his feet, leaning back against the cupboards as he drew Hope up into his embrace, sliding his arms around her, slanting his mouth over hers to deepen the kiss. Hope let her lips part, shivering at the new sensations he was showing her, drowning in feelings.

It was the bump on her head that brought her back to reality. When the car from behind had plowed into her, her head had banged back against the padded headrest, which hadn't felt very padded at that moment. It had undoubtedly saved her from whiplash, just as it was meant to do, but it had left her with a good-sized bump on the back of her skull. When Sean slid his long, strong fingers into her hair to cradle her head, his hand slipped across the bump. Hope came back down to earth with a jolt.

"Ooh!" She jerked back, reaching up automatically to cover the sharp ache with her hand.

"What's the matter?" Sean's question was quick, and as sharp as the pain in her skull. When she didn't answer quickly enough, he repeated it. "What's wrong, Hope? What is it!"

"Just my head." She turned away, still with her hand over the bump, hiding her face from him. The ache in her head was minor compared to the embarrassed chagrin flooding through her.

"What's the matter with your head?" Oblivious to her embarrassment, Sean caught her elbow, gently this time, and turned her back to face him.

"I've got a bump," Hope admitted.

"Where?" Sean lifted her hand from her head and slipped his fingers lightly, delicately, through her hair. He found the spot with his fingertips, and she winced.

"That's it, but don't press too hard, okay?"

She tried to twist her head away, but he didn't let her, though his touch went from merely delicate to feather light.

"Whoa. Hold still. You've got a real goose egg there, don't you? What happened?"

"My head banged on the headrest when that guy hit me."

"I thought those headrests were supposed to be padded."

"So did I."

"Did you tell the cop you were hurt?"

Hope shook her head, and regretted it immediately. She closed her eyes, willing the ache to subside. "There was no reason to. It's just a bump on the head."

"You ought to see a doctor."

"Don't be silly. It's just a little bump. By tomorrow I won't even know it's there."

"It's not little. That's one hell of a bump."

"But that's all it is. Just a bump."

"All right," he said grudgingly after a moment. "I guess. Were you hurt anywhere else?"

"I had on my seat belt." Hope moved a step away, and Sean let his hand fall to his side again. "Seat belts do work, you know," she reminded him.

"I know they do, but you could be in shock or something. Look..." He glanced over his shoulder at the microwave. "Instead of flinging accusations around and arguing about every little thing, just sit down at the table while I get some dinner together, will you?"

Happy enough to put a little distance between them, Hope nodded assent and retreated to the kitchen table with unaccustomed meekness. Sean didn't need to worry about her. In fact his concern, after his kiss, made her uncomfortable. Just as his kiss, after his accusations, had made her uncomfortable. Just as his accusations had hurt her deeply.

Of course she had been, as Sean pointed out, hurling a few accusations of her own. No wonder he was angry. Whatever she believed, and she wasn't even sure what she believed anymore, she should never have said the things she'd said. Sean had every right and more than enough reason to toss her out on her ear and refuse to let her back in his house. Or to refuse to let her work on Whitey's papers ever again. Hope turned in her chair, away from Sean, who was working between the refrigerator and the microwave, and stared bleakly out the window at the rapidly gathering dusk.

"Sean, I'm all right. I really am."

"You're not." He steered her across the living room to a sofa and gently, but irresistibly, pushed her down. He lifted her feet onto a brocade footstool and grabbed a needlepoint pillow from an armchair next to the sofa. "Here. Put this behind your head."

"I'm not going to—"

"Just put it there, okay?"

He glowered and she sighed, exasperated.

"All right." She tucked the pillow behind her head and glowered back. "Satisfied?"

"For the time being." He turned away to pour a cup of coffee, adding one spoonful of sugar and a little milk, then turned back to hand it to Hope before pouring his own.

She sipped, and was perversely annoyed to find he'd fixed it just right, exactly the way she liked it. That shouldn't have irritated her, but it did.

"I feel silly," she announced.

"Why?" Sean asked idly. He sipped his own coffee, black and scalding.

"Because you're treating me like an invalid, and I'm not. I'm fine and I'd like to go do some more work on the papers. And anyway—" she swung her feet off the footstool and straightened, setting aside the needle-point pillow "—all this coddling is embarrassing!"

Sean caught her hand before she could rise, keeping her on the sofa. "Just sit still, can't you?"

"No, I can't." She pulled free of his hand. "You've fed me lovely Thai leftovers for dinner and made me sit and rest, and given me coffee and treated me like a critical case. I don't want you to get the impression that I don't appreciate it, but—"

"But you don't appreciate it," Sean interrupted.

"I just . . . I don't like to be smothered," she admitted. "I'm not used to it. It makes me uncomfortable."

"Because you've spent most of your life being the one who takes care of someone else? Your father, your students?"

"I didn't mind taking care of my father," she said quickly, defensively. "I *wanted* to take care of him."

"I'm not saying you didn't, or that you shouldn't have. What you did was admirable, commendable." Sean moved from the chair he'd taken to the sofa, beside her. "All I'm saying is that maybe it's your turn now."

"My turn?"

"To be taken care of. Maybe it's time you let somebody take care of you for a change."

She shrugged. "I feel like a fraud. I was just in a little fender bender. My car got banged up, but all I got was a bump on the head and a bruised shoulder from the shoulder belt."

"A bruise?" he demanded, snapping out of his lethargy. "You didn't tell me you had anything but that bump."

"There's nothing to tell. The belt held me in the seat, that's all."

"Where's the bruise?" Sean took her shoulders very gently and turned her to face him. "Let me see. It ought to have ice on it or something."

"Sean, it's only a bruise. It's nothing—"

"Just let me see it." He didn't hold her tightly, didn't seem to be using any force at all, but Hope found she couldn't move away, couldn't seem to resist as he turned her on the cushions until she faced him fully.

He studied her for a moment, thinking aloud to amuse and distract her. "You were driving, so it would have to be your left shoulder... unless you were driving an English car, but they never sold anything that big in England unless it was for hauling furniture, so it has to be your left shoulder."

Hope was smiling at his silliness, but her smile faded when he reached out for the first button of her blouse. She stiffened, reaching up to catch his wrist.

"Let me see it, Hope."

It would be futile to resist. She could see that in his face, hear it in his quiet, determined words. Slowly she took her hand away, averting her face, staring at the far wall. Her blouse was cotton lawn, with a wide, eyelet-trimmed collar and pearly buttons. He quickly unfastened the first four of those pearl buttons.

He pushed the blouse off her shoulder, then her camisole strap, and swore under his breath at what he saw.

"Why the hell didn't you tell me about this? It needed ice on it right after it happened."

Hope closed her eyes as his fingertips slid lightly over her skin from the top of her shoulder down to the edge of her camisole, where it rested on the upper curve of her breast.

"That has to hurt," he said quietly.

"Not much," she whispered. "Only a little."

"It looks like it hurts." He slipped his arms around her with exquisite gentleness and gathered her close. "At first I was irritated that you were late, you know. You're never late, even when the traffic's bad. I was mad at first, but then I started getting scared, started thinking about what could have happened. So I went to look for you. And then I saw that accident . . ."

He tightened his arms around her, buried his face in her hair. "I don't know what I thought when I saw that, but—"

"Don't." Hope lifted her arms and laid them lightly around his shoulders. "Sean, don't, please." She patted his shoulder a little awkwardly, feeling the rocklike tension in his muscles. "I'm okay. I'm fine, and there's nothing to worry about except how long it will take the garage to get my car fixed."

Seconds ticked past as he sat with his face in her hair. Then he sighed heavily. "I know. I know you're okay." His shoulders shook a little as he chuckled. "I guess now that I know you're okay I can get mad at you for scaring me that way."

"Oh, goody."

He chuckled again and lifted his head. "I ought to warn you, about fifty percent of what comes out of your mouth makes me mad. I don't know what it is, but you can make me crazy faster than just about anybody I know."

"How did I get so lucky?"

"Just be being you, I guess." He ran his hands over her back. "By being sweet and feisty and shy and smart and pushy and obsessed with this crazy quest of yours."

Hope shook her head, smiling ruefully. "I don't sound like much of a bargain, do I?"

Sean frowned quizzically. "I might have left something out," he said softly.

"Like what?" Hope whispered.

"Oh, like fascinating." Sean bent his head to brush his lips over her cheek. "Or beautiful." He lifted his head for a moment, then bent again. "Especially beautiful," he breathed, and captured her mouth.

The kiss went on and on, deep and searching, seeking the response she couldn't have hidden if she'd wanted to. She could feel his need, and could feel that it was more than sexual, though certainly passion figured prominently in it. He needed to reassure himself that she was all right, unhurt, alive and whole and warm in his arms.

Hope sought to give him the reassurance he needed. She held him and kissed him and knew the exact mo-

ment when his embrace changed, and passion replaced
the need for reassurance.

He shifted his embrace, pulling her across his lap,
cradling her in the curve of his arm while his other hand
restlessly roamed her back, stroking up and down her
spine, tangling in her hair as he pulled her mouth up to
his, then stroking down her spine again.

Hope lay pliant in his arms, clinging to his shoulders
as her breath came quick and short and her head began
to spin. When he unfastened another button on her
blouse, she didn't flinch, and when he slipped his hand
inside, beneath the hem of her camisole, to caress her
skin, she welcomed this new closeness.

He stroked her back, her ribs and waist, then drew his
hand up, slowly, to rest just below her breast. Hope
caught her breath, her heart hammering in her chest,
and for a moment she went very still. Sean was as still
as she, waiting, allowing her time to withdraw from
further intimacies.

She didn't withdraw. Instead, she pressed closer,
arching her back, inviting his caress. And when his
palm slid over her breast, she shivered at the new and
unexpected sensations flooding her. His caressing hand
was gentle, but his touch seemed to scorch her skin, and
she could feel her breast swell into his hand, her nipple
pucker to a tight, aching bud.

Her body was burning, her skin was hot, and there
was a hollow ache low in her belly. She couldn't ease
that ache, only Sean could, and for one blind moment
she didn't care about anything else.

But if she was lost to this newly discovered passion,
Sean was not, not quite. He knew what was happening
and where it was leading, and he knew they had to stop,

now, because he was dangerously close to the point at which stopping would be impossible.

Hope felt his withdrawal and clung blindly with a little whimper of protest, tightening her arms around his neck, seeking his lips when he drew away. Sean groaned aloud when she found his mouth with her sweet, inexperienced lips, but still he twisted his face away, took his hand from her breast and pressed her face into his shoulder, holding her while he mastered himself.

"Sean?"

"Shh." He pressed a quick kiss onto her hair, then set her gently off his lap, taking her clinging hands from his shoulders and clasping them between his own. "Shh. It's okay."

She swallowed hard, shaking a little, and turned away, huddling on the cushions. Sean reached to comfort her, but she shook off his hand. Now that he was no longer kissing her or holding her, she was coldly, humiliatingly aware of what they'd been doing, what *she'd* been doing.

She glanced at Sean, then looked quickly away when she saw his shirt, pulled askew by her caressing hands. Her state of dress was no better, her blouse undone and her camisole pulled free of her waistband. Her hair was wildly mussed, and she was breathless and shaking with unfulfilled desire.

And she was filled with the scalding shame of knowing that if Sean hadn't had enough control—not to mention good sense—to stop them when he had, that desire would not have gone unfulfilled.

She'd never known, never even suspected, that desire could be such a monumental force, powerful enough to sweep away sense and reason and sixteen years of convent education. All those things had counted for nothing when she was in Sean's arms, with his hands on her body, his lips kissing hers.

Hope had learned she was capable of wantonness, and it wasn't a comfortable discovery. She'd always imagined that lovemaking would follow courtship and falling in love and marrying, yet without Sean's self-control that evening, she'd have had the intimacy with neither courting nor love nor marriage.

She'd known Sean Boudreaux only a few short weeks. She'd had a vicious argument with him just that evening. She'd admitted she didn't trust him, just as he didn't trust her. And yet she'd have made love with him.

She dropped her head, letting her hair swing forward to hide her burning face, and tried with shaking fingers to straighten her disordered clothing.

"Give me the number of that police garage and I'll call them in the morning." Sean spoke from the sofa beside her, but she didn't turn around to look at him.

"A-all right." Hope couldn't seem to keep her voice from shaking.

"I'll drive you home tonight and get a cab back here. You can keep my car till yours is fixed."

At that, Hope looked around. "Keep the Triumph?"

"Actually," he replied with something that was almost a chuckle, "I meant the BMW, since it's a sedan, but if you'd rather have the Triumph—"

"No. Oh, no! The BMW is more than generous, it's too much. I can't let you do that. I'll just rent a car until mine is fixed."

"Does your car insurance cover rentals?"

"I don't know. Should it?"

"Not necessarily. You usually have to add that coverage specially. And since rental cars cost a fortune,

you'll just have to borrow mine. I'll feel better knowing you have a decent car to drive instead of some
junker rental."

Hope hesitated, then nodded, capitulating. She had
her pride, but she also had to be realistic. She couldn't
afford to rent a car for two or three weeks, but she
needed a car to get to work. "All right. Thank you."

"Are you ready to go?"

"But I haven't done any work on the papers at all."

"Don't worry about it. You were in a car accident. I
don't think anybody would disagree that that's a good
enough reason to take the night off."

"I suppose so." Hope looked down the hall toward
Whitey's office. "I feel like I should do something,
though."

"Don't worry about it," he repeated, and started toward the door. "Come on. You need some sleep."

Hope abandoned argument and went with him.

Not that he gave her a choice. That realization came
to Hope as she lay in bed waiting for sleep. Wanting her
to get home and get some sleep was perfectly reasonable, but Sean had practically hustled her out of his
house. He'd driven fast on the way to her home, then
waited impatiently for the cab to arrive to take him
away. It was as if, she realized, he couldn't get away
from her quickly enough.

What had happened? Between the time he took her
to his house and cared for her with such thoroughness
and the time he hustled her out of his house, what had
happened?

She knew the answer to that; it was obvious. Sean
had kissed her, and their embrace had nearly gotten out
of hand. And something about that had prompted him
to hurry her out of his house and away from him.

Had he found her unattractive? Had she done something wrong, been too forward or too inexperienced? What had happened?

The question was both humiliating and unanswerable, but the conclusion was obvious. Sean had kissed her and found her so lacking in some way that he couldn't wait to get her away from his house, away from him.

And that hurt, more than she'd have believed possible.

Hope quickly punched out five digits on the phone, paused, pressed a sixth, hesitated, then dropped the receiver quickly back onto its rest.

It was silly to be afraid of a simple phone call. The message from Sean had come just after noon, when she was busy with her class and couldn't come to the phone. The yellow message slip had said only that Sean had a meeting that night and she needn't come to work on the papers.

She needed to talk to him, if only to reassure herself that he wasn't seriously angry with her, but when she finally gathered her nerve and dialed his number, all she got was his answering machine. Her carefully worded message was brief and impersonal, until the end. "When you get in," she concluded, her voice just a little too thin, a little too high, "could you call me? Please?"

But her phone didn't ring. It didn't ring that night or the next, and when she called to see what was going on, she again reached only his machine. She left a cool little message this time, keeping any hint of an emotional quaver out of her voice.

She'd have liked simply to ignore the obstinate silence of her phone, but that wasn't easy. She tried to keep herself busy with make-work tasks, but she couldn't stop herself from leaping for the phone when it rang at eight that evening.

"Sean? Is that you?" She clutched the receiver tightly. "Is anything wrong?"

"Good evening," said an oddly toneless male voice. "I'm Mike, a computer, and I'd like to offer you the vacation opportunity of a lifetime."

"What in the world—" Hope yanked the receiver away from her ear, glared at it, then banged it down. "I *hate* those things! Vacation opportunity, my eye!" She returned to cleaning the crisper drawer in her refrigerator, occasionally glancing at the silent phone and muttering in disgust.

She endured three days of answering machines and unreturned messages, then gave up. If she couldn't speak to him on the phone, then she'd go and see him. Not that she needed a reason after three days of unanswered messages, but there might be something wrong. Maybe there was something she could help with. Or Sean might need his car back.

Most importantly, of course, she wanted to get back to work on the papers. She had to find some proof of her father's authorship of those screenplays, and she couldn't afford to allow her increasingly complicated relationship with Sean to get in the way of that goal.

When she left school on the fourth day, she hurried home to change, then drove fast towards Sean's house, taking a slightly guilty pleasure in the BMW's power and comfort. She didn't like being beholden to Sean, but she had to admit that she was going to miss the BMW when her car was finally repaired. She pulled up before his front door with a flourish, set the brake, climbed out and marched up the steps to the front door.

The first ring of Whitey's incredible doorbell brought no response, nor did the second, so for the third ring, she just leaned on the button and listened to Big Ben pealing thunderously in the distance, over and over and—

"For God's sake, let up on that button!" A furious Sean flung the door open and grabbed Hope's wrist, yanking her hand off the button. "What are you trying to do, ruin my hearing?"

"No." Hope shook her head. "I'm trying to get your attention."

"My ears are still ringing." He shook his head, scowling, then looked at Hope, seeming to really notice her for the first time. "Hope?" She could see him stiffen into uneasiness. "What are you doing here?" He straightened and looked past her at the canyon and the hills.

"I told you. I'm getting your attention."

"What?"

"Getting your attention. I can't reach you by phone, you won't answer my messages, so I came out here, where you can't ignore me."

"Oh." He was studying the familiar canyon vista with unusual intensity. "I've ... I've been busy."

"That wouldn't bother me. I'm perfectly capable of working on the papers while you have your meetings and things."

He shrugged without meeting her eyes. "It just didn't seem like a good idea, with being busy and all."

"Well, are you busy now?"

He shrugged again. "I've got a lot of work ..."

"You won't even know I'm here."

"Hope, it's not really a good—"

"I see." She cut him off, her heart sinking as she suddenly realized what he was trying to say. "I'll go."

"Wait a minute!" He caught her arm as she turned away. "What do you mean, you see? What do you see?"

Hope looked back at him, her face set. "I see why you don't want me here if you're busy."

"You do, do you? And just why is that?"

She turned away. "Because you don't trust me."

Chapter 6

"I what?"

"You don't trust me," she repeated, still turned away. There was a pause.

"I don't what?"

"Trust me. You said so, after all."

"I see."

"And now I understand. You've been busy, so you weren't free to work in Whitey's study when I did, and since you don't want me working in there alone, you told me not to come."

"I did, huh?"

"It's obvious, isn't it?"

He shrugged. "At the risk of being ungentlemanly, I might point out that you said you didn't trust me, either."

She turned slowly to face him but wouldn't meet his eyes. "I had no right to say that. I apologize."

"You had as much right as I did. And probably about as much reason. Come on." He took her hand and pushed the door wide for her. "As long as you're here, you might as well get some sorting done."

"Really?" she asked.

"Yeah. Really." His voice was abrupt, but he led her into the house. Not to the study, though, but to the kitchen. "Have you had dinner?"

"Well, no."

"Neither have I. You want Chinese or pizza?"

"I—" Hope shook her head helplessly. "Whatever you're having is fine."

"Pizza, then." He picked up the phone. "Everything but anchovies?"

"Actually I like anchovies. I can't face pineapple on pizza, though."

"Everything but pineapple, then." He dialed the number quickly without having to look it up, gave his order and was nodding with satisfaction when he hung up. "They'll be here in about forty-five minutes. Want to work until then?"

She did, of course, but back in the now familiar study, where she was sure nothing had been touched since the last time she'd worked there nearly a week before, Hope had trouble concentrating.

Everything was as it had been, yet nothing was the same. She still sat at Whitey's massive desk, and Sean still sat at his table across the room, but things were different now. Words had been said that couldn't be unsaid. Hurtful allegations had been hurled and reciprocated. Kisses and caresses had been exchanged, and neither of them could forget.

Hope was intensely aware of Sean, of the long silences while he thought, of the bursts of rapid typing, the occasional mutters of annoyance or satisfaction at what he'd written. She was aware, even without looking, when he glanced across the room at her, and she could feel the quick heat in her cheeks, the sudden self-consciousness of her movements.

Something else was different, too. Sean was there in the room with her, but there was a distance between them despite the heightened awareness. Something was wrong, and it wasn't her imagination.

Sean had been avoiding her. She hadn't mistaken his dismay and irritation when she appeared on his doorstep this afternoon. He'd been avoiding her, and he had not been pleased when she showed up. There had to be a reason for it, some reason why he hadn't returned her phone calls, why he'd told her to stay away from his house, why he'd been annoyed to see her there.

Unfortunately, she thought she had a pretty good idea what his reason was, and it didn't make her any happier. She looked at Sean, typing with machine-gun speed, his gaze intent on the small computer screen, a lock of hair falling onto his forehead. Her hand itched to push it back, to feel once again how soft and thick his hair was. She stifled the urge, pulled her gaze away and focused it again on the work in front of her. This was what was important, this was why she was here. To find the proof of her father's talent, of his work. Not to moon over Sean Boudreaux like a lovesick teenager.

She flipped open the next folder and for twenty minutes read her way doggedly through a stack of sarcastic memos from Whitey to one of the producers at his studio. She read the memos with grim determination and none of the enjoyment she usually found in Whitey's acerbic humor. She carefully didn't look at Sean again, and in due time the doorbell rang, signaling the arrival of dinner.

They took the pizza and sodas out to the patio, where a warm breeze was blowing, the beginning of a Santa Ana wind. Hope knew it would be howling around the eaves by tomorrow, raising the temperature to over one hundred, scorching landscaping and fraying tempers. For the moment, though, the wind from the desert to the northeast was still a breeze, and the temperature was still balmy, not roasting.

Hope let the warmth soothe her, let the food fortify her, and when she was finished eating, she gathered her courage and sat up in her chair and asked what she was afraid to ask.

Sean had moved from the table and the small circle of light cast by a camping lantern in the center of it when he'd finished eating. He was standing in the dark by the low wall that separated the patio from the hillside. Hope moved to the wall, a few feet away, and stood there looking out into the night.

"Sean?" She spoke softly, and there was a moment's pause before he answered.

"Hmm?"

"Could you—" She paused. "Could you tell me what is wrong?"

He turned his head to look over at her, but she couldn't see his face in the darkness. "Tell you what?"

"What's wrong. Something obviously is. Can't you tell me what?"

He looked away again. "There's nothing to tell."

"I wish you wouldn't patronize me, Sean. I know you think I'm hopelessly naive, but I'm not stupid. Something changed the other day, after—" She hesitated, swallowing hard. "After you kissed me. I very much wish you'd tell me what it is."

"Can you just leave it alone, Hope?"

"No." She spoke quietly but with conviction, giving him the part of the truth that she could tell him. "No, I can't leave it alone. If for no other reason than the fact that I'm only here to work on sufferance. If you decide to withdraw your permission because something's gone wrong between you and me, I'll never finish the work on the papers, and I'll never do what I have to do."

Sean finally turned around, leaning back against the stone wall and folding his arms across his chest. "Why all the rush, Hope? Why do you *have* to come every day and work on those papers? Why all this desperate hurry?"

"Because I've waited too long already. It's something I have to do, Sean. It's for my father. You understand that, don't you?"

"No, I don't, if you want to know the truth," he told her after a moment. "I don't understand it."

"He's my *father.*"

"So?"

"So I loved him. So I want to honor him with the truth about his work. So this is more important to me than anything else."

"Just because he was your father."

"Yes. Of course." Hope watched him closely. She could see grimness in his face and a hint of anger, but no sign at all that he understood what she was saying. "You're writing a book about your father, Sean. You must understand why I'm doing this."

He shook his head, quick and short. "I'm not writing the book to *glorify* my father, Hope. I'm writing it to set the record straight, to tell the truth."

"But you're writing about him because you know him better than anyone else. You're writing it because you love him." It was somewhere between a suggestion and a question.

Sean shook his head in sharp denial. "You're wrong, Hope. That's not why I'm writing it at all."

He turned away and Hope stared at his straight back and stiff shoulders while long seconds of silence ticked by. When she spoke, her voice was low and gentle.

"Why are you writing the book, Sean?"

"Maybe because someone else will, if I don't. Maybe to exorcise a few demons. Maybe because I *didn't* know my father better than anyone else." He turned around, watching her face. "Maybe I'm writing it because I hardly knew him at all."

"How could you not? He was your father!"

"Yeah. He was. And I didn't have any contact with him at all for the last ten years of his life!"

Hope stared, openmouthed and shocked.

"Well?" Sean demanded, almost angrily. "Aren't you going to ask me about it? Don't you want to know why I didn't see my father for ten years? Don't you want to know what happened? Don't you want all the gory details?"

She shook her head. "You don't have to tell me anything, Sean. You owe me nothing, certainly not an explanation."

Some tension deep within him suddenly seemed to ease. He sighed heavily, and the anger left his face. "I'm not so sure I don't." He caught Hope's hand. "Come over here and sit down."

He led her across the patio, and when she was seated on a glider, he slumped in a chair facing her, elbows on his knees, his hands dangling between them. He was silent for a long time, while the breeze rustled the fronds of a fan palm beside the house and teased the ends of Hope's hair so that they drifted across her face.

"You were right," he said without looking at her.

Hope straightened and pushed her hair back off her face, but she didn't speak.

"I was avoiding you. I did have a meeting that first night, but after that, it seemed easier to avoid your phone calls, to be alone, than to have you come back and make me see things I didn't want to see." He glanced at her, then looked back down at his hands. "I'm not proud of it, but I had my reasons." When she still said nothing, he looked up. "Well? Aren't you going to ask what my reasons are?"

"No. It's not my place to ask. You'll tell me what you want me to know."

Sean grimaced. "I don't deserve that kind of consideration, Hope. I think I'd feel better if you yelled at me like you did the other night."

She shook her head. "Yelling won't solve anything, will it? It certainly didn't the other night."

"Good point," he acknowledged with a wry grin. "You're right, again. Yelling doesn't solve anything, and I was avoiding you. I was..." He looked up at the darkening sky, then down at his hands. "This is going to shoot my macho image, such as it is, all to hell, but I was scared."

"Scared? Of what?"

"Of things...that were getting out of hand."

"Oh." Hope looked away, biting her lip.

"Hey, don't look like that. If you're thinking that—"

"That I behaved badly," she said quietly, then squeaked in surprise when he caught her wrist and pulled her forward to face him nose to nose.

"Don't say that!" he ordered. "Don't say it. Don't even think it! You did nothing wrong, nothing. I did, and I wasn't trying to punish you for my mistake. I just needed distance. Do you understand that?"

She didn't really, but she nodded, and he released her wrist so she could sit back.

He watched her for a moment, then leaned back in his chair and looked away, out into the night.

"Maybe I felt I needed a little distance from you because my feelings about you... for you... are far from simple. You charged into my life, full of fire and determination, with a story that still sounds too fantastic to be true." He glanced at her, at her expression. "I'm sorry to be so blunt, Hope, but you've got to understand how hard it still is for me to believe that whole story."

He waited until she nodded again before going on.

"Anyway, you marched in with this wild story, talking about your father, how close you were to him, how you loved him and admired him. You told me how he took care of you when you were little, and how you took care of him when he was old and sick. It all meant so much to you, but I didn't have any idea what you were talking about."

She must have made some sound or movement of protest, for he nodded.

"It's true. The kind of father-child relationship you talk about isn't something I can even imagine. I had a father, but I never had that kind of relationship with him. For most of my life I didn't really have a relationship with him at all. He and my mother divorced when

I was five. I lived in this house before the divorce, but my only real memory of the first five years of my life is of one Christmas, when I was four, I think. There was a tree in the living room, one of those designer Christmas trees. You know the kind I mean, all white with all blue ornaments, and about twenty feet tall. I wasn't allowed to touch it.

"When we finally opened the gifts, I couldn't wait to get to the one from my dad. It was in this great big box, so I figured it had to be a terrific present, but when I opened it, it was a typewriter." He shook his head. "Maybe if I'd been a college freshman I'd have appreciated it, but what I wanted was a fire truck. I was four years old, too young to be tactful, to pretend an enthusiasm I didn't feel. My father knew I didn't like his present, and I knew my father was disappointed in me."

Hope reached out to touch his hand. "I'm sorry you had to be disappointed that way, Sean. It must have hurt."

He shrugged. "If anything, that was the high point of my relationship with my father."

"But you must have seen him after the divorce."

"Yeah, I saw him. For a weekend a month, and a couple of weeks in the summer. If he was in town. If he wasn't off somewhere working. And if he and whoever his wife was at the time didn't have plans that didn't include a kid of seven or eight." He paused. "I saw him maybe four or five times a year until I was seventeen and we had the big blowup."

"What happened?" she asked quietly, watching him in the dim light slanting out through the windows.

"I was here on a weekend visit. Whitey was getting ready for his wedding to wife number four, calling caterers, trying to buy a ring that was even bigger than the one he'd bought for wife number three. He asked me how I liked her." Sean gave a humorless chuckle, his face bleak. "I was young and self-righteous, and I hadn't learned too much about tact since that Christmas when I was four, so I told him what I thought."

"Which was?"

"That she was an empty-headed, hard-hearted, bleached-blond, gold-digging bitch."

"Oh."

Sean almost smiled. "Yeah. Oh. I was too big to be spanked by that time. I was about three inches taller than Whitey, as a matter of fact, so instead of spanking me, he broke my nose." He glanced at Hope's shocked face, then away. "I said some things that he couldn't forgive, he said some things that I couldn't forgive, and I didn't see him again for ten years."

"But you did see him again?"

He nodded. "I think we'd both regretted that fight, but neither of us would unbend enough to make the first move until something happened to force us to. I read in the paper that Whitey had been admitted to the cancer unit at Cedars-Sinai Medical Center, and a couple of days later I got a call from his lawyer saying that he wanted to see me. I wasn't sure I really wanted to see him, but in the end, I went."

"What happened?"

"It's more a question of what didn't happen. There was no tear-jerking, big-screen reconciliation scene. We were just as awkward with each other as we'd always been. Neither of us quite knew what to say. We were both on edge, as always, ready to take offense at any poorly phrased remark. It took a couple of weeks for us to even get around to talking about the fight that drove us apart in the first place. Of course, by that time

Whitey had long since divorced the gold digger in question and married and divorced wife number five."

He tossed Hope a wry smile. "He admitted that I'd been fairly accurate in my assessment of her, and I admitted that, accurate or not, I'd had no right at seventeen to criticize my father's choice of a wife."

"I'm glad you had that chance."

"I am, too, but that doesn't mean I don't have regrets. We lost so many years, years that we could have known each other as adults, and we could never get those back. He was terminally ill, and we only had a few weeks before he died. You can't get back the past. You can't recapture ten years in a few weeks." He looked up. "So now you understand why I don't know much of anything about Whitey's business, including any business he might have had with your father."

"You had that time together, though," she suggested. "You had time to talk."

"So did he say anything about Philip Carruthers?" Sean completed her unasked question. "No, he didn't. We talked, but not about things like his work."

"I'd have thought, though, when he knew it was your last chance—"

"Exactly. We talked about the things that seemed most important at the time. We made our peace, but it didn't seem crucial to share all the details of life stories."

"I see. And I can understand. Details don't seem very important at a time like that."

"No, they don't. So can you see now why I can't give you much information about Whitey's life and work? I can't tell you what I don't know." He smiled. "I know what you thought, though."

"What I thought?"

"Yeah. You thought I was lying to you for devious reasons of my own, right?"

"Of course not, Sean. I—" She saw the skepticism plain in his face and sighed. "Well, maybe I did suspect you were lying to me, once, for a moment or two. Mostly I just wondered what you were trying to hide from me, and why."

"I wasn't hiding anything," he said. "Except—" He stopped.

"Except what?" Hope prompted after a moment.

"Except that I could see the kind of relationship you had with your father, how close you were. I couldn't help being jealous of that. You and your father had a wonderful relationship, and I didn't want to admit to you that my father and I barely had a relationship at all."

"But there's nothing for you to feel ashamed of, Sean. It's sad that it happened, but it's not your fault."

"Then why do I feel guilty?"

"Maybe it's human nature to feel guilty about things that aren't in our power to change."

"Maybe," he replied, unconvinced. "Maybe."

"There is something you can do, though."

"Oh, yeah?" He leaned back in his chair, watching her through the darkness. "What's that?"

"You've already started it, with the biography of Whitey. You can learn everything there is to know about your father and his life. You'll come to know him and understand him, even though he isn't here any longer. Aren't you looking forward to knowing the truth? Once and for all?"

"Oh, God." He sighed deeply, sliding down in the chair until he was looking up at the stars pricking the indigo dome of the night sky overhead. "I don't know.

I want to know the truth, and yet I'm not sure the myth and the illusion wouldn't be easier to live with than the reality."

"It probably would be easier...if you didn't know it was illusion. You're too intelligent to settle for less than the truth, Sean."

"That, or just too damn nosy." He looked over at her. "You know, at first I didn't think there was anything more to know. I dismissed you and your cocka-mamy story out of hand."

"And now?" Hope wondered, watching his face intently.

"Now I think I have to know the truth, whatever it is."

Relief washed through her in an almost physical tide. "Then you'll let me keep going through the papers?"

"If you want to, yes."

"Thank you, Sean."

"Don't thank me. It's a hell of a job."

"I was just afraid," Hope blurted, "after the other evening—" She stopped herself suddenly before she went any further.

"After the other evening, what?" Sean asked. "After I kissed you?"

Hope bit her lip, then nodded.

"You were afraid because I kissed you." He shoved himself out of the chair and walked a couple of steps away from her, away from the light slanting out the kitchen windows and into the darkness. "I know it doesn't count for much, but I apologize for that. I should have known it would scare you."

Hope got up and followed him into the shadows at the edge of the patio, stopping a pace away from him. "The kisses didn't scare me, Sean."

Her voice was very soft, but he heard every word. He pushed his fists into his pockets, hunching his shoulders. "You said you were afraid," he reminded her, still looking away, out at the canyon and the hills. "What were you afraid of, then?"

"I was afraid..." Hope faltered. This time it was she who turned away, hiding her face. "You hurried me home that day, and then you wouldn't call me or talk to me. I was afraid that...that I'd done something wrong. That I'd disgusted you, and you didn't want me around anymore."

The bricks grated beneath Sean's shoes as he pivoted slowly to face her. Hope glanced at him but could see only his silhouette against the lights inside. His face was in shadow, and she could read nothing there.

"Is that what you think?" he asked, very softly. "That you disgusted me?"

She moved her head and shoulders in a silent admission.

"How could you ever imagine you could do that?"

She shrugged miserably. "What was I to think?" she whispered. "You kissed me, and then... It was so obvious that you didn't want me around... What was I to think?"

"That I was a jerk!" he whispered explosively. "That I'd let things get out of hand, and I was punishing myself by keeping you away." He reached out to catch her wrist and draw her closer. "I was disgusted, you were right about that, but with myself, not you. You did nothing wrong."

"Then why did you push me away that way? Why didn't you tell me what was going on? I was worried that—" She stopped herself before she said too much. "I didn't know what to think."

"I know." He touched her cheek lightly, then released her wrist, stepping back. "And I'm sorry for that. I thought we needed a little space, a little time away from each other. We needed some time alone."

Hope frowned. "I'm sure your motives were admirable, but don't you think you might have talked to me before you made this unilateral decision for *our* good?"

Sean looked down his nose at her. "I did what I thought was right."

"I imagine you did, but it wasn't right." Hope faced him squarely, her small chin set at a defiant angle. "As a matter of fact, I really think it was presumptuous, and high-handed, and—"

"Hope, you don't know what—"

"No!" she interrupted. "I think it's you who doesn't know. You're patronizing me, Sean, and I don't see any reason to put up with it. I may not be as sophisticated as you, but that's hardly a reason for you to treat me like the village idiot!"

"Hope, I am not treating you like an idiot!"

"Aren't you?" she demanded. "I know I'm not as worldly and cynical as you, Sean. I even know that makes me naive in your eyes, but it doesn't mean I'm stupid. I can deal with reality. I've dealt with plenty of reality in my life, and I won't have you assuming I need to be shielded from it like some hothouse flower."

Sean studied her face in the uncertain light. After a few moments he nodded, acknowledging what she'd said.

"All right. You're right. Maybe I've been trying to protect you from something you don't need protection from."

"So will you tell me why you wouldn't answer my messages?"

"Yeah." He stepped back, putting a little distance between them, raked a hand roughly through his hair and cleared his throat. "I thought we needed some space, some distance between us, because..."

He rubbed a hand over his face, looked up at the sky as if seeking an answer from the stars, then lowered his gaze to Hope again. "Because I was spooked. Hell, I was scared! We didn't just kiss the other night, Hope. We came damned close to making love on the sofa in my living room, and that would have been one hell of a mistake."

"But, Sean, we—"

"You're a virgin." He cut her off. "Aren't you?"

She bit her lip, but she didn't deny it.

"That's right," he said. "You're a convent-school virgin, and I— Well, let's just say I'm not." He rubbed a hand around the back of his neck. "We don't have a damned thing in common except some old business that you tell me our fathers had together. If you want to keep coming here to work on the papers, and if I'm going to let you, we can't make any more mistakes like that. We can work together on these papers, but only if we can keep our relationship professional. Just professional."

"I see," Hope said quietly, torn between relief and a hurt that went deep, far deeper than she'd have imagined it would. She was a virgin, and so Sean didn't want her. He'd kissed her, but he obviously hadn't felt the same things she had. Her eyes suddenly burned with unshed tears, and she turned away, blindly grabbing the pizza box to carry it into the kitchen.

It didn't matter, she told herself fiercely. It *didn't!* She hadn't come to Sean to act out some stupid, ro-

mantic daydream, but for the sake of her father's reputation.

Sean was going to allow her to keep working on the
papers, and that was all that mattered. Or so she told
herself.

Chapter 7

Sean felt like a heel. He felt as if he'd just taken candy from a baby. And kicked a defenseless puppy, just for good measure. Long after Hope had left for the evening, driving away in his BMW, he could still see the hurt in her big green eyes, could still see the way they'd darkened from emerald to a smoky sea green when he brought up the fact of her virginity.

"Damn it!" He threw his jeans inside the closet and slammed the door hard in frustration. He hadn't wanted to be cruel to her. It felt wrong, even though he knew it had been the only decent thing to do.

Better to hurt Hope now than to let things go on until he hurt her far more. For she would get hurt in the end, of that he was sure.

Hope thought she was falling for him. Sean couldn't let that go on. He had to nip it in the bud. She wasn't the type of girl who had affairs. She'd expect marriage. Hell, she'd deserve it. The next thing he knew, she'd be talking about white dresses and bouquets, expecting a ring and a proposal. But Sean wasn't marrying, not her, not anyone.

He wasn't falling into that trap another time. Seven years ago, when his marriage went up in flames, he had sworn to himself that he'd never walk down the aisle and back into that kind of hell again.

Hope did her best to ignore the hurt of Sean's rejection and to concentrate on her search for the truth, but it was frustratingly slow going. She sorted and searched through box after box, file after file stuffed with papers, working until her eyes would no longer focus, six or seven nights a week. Though she discovered all sorts of interesting things, read fascinating script fragments and hilarious letters, she found nothing at all concerning Philip Carruthers.

At first, she'd been borne on a wave of excitement that seemed to swell anew each time she opened another box or file. Each time, she'd hoped that this one would be *the* one, the box that would hold letters from Philip to Whitey, the file that would contain a screenplay with Philip's handwritten notes on it, the drawer where she'd find an old ledger that would prove to the world that Philip Carruthers had been a genius. Time passed, though, and box after file after drawer yielded nothing, and the bright glow of hope began to lose its luster.

It seemed the more she searched, the less she found, and the longer she went on, the more frustrated she became, the more desperate to find the answer she sought. And the more desperate she became, the more Sean worried about her.

"Want to take a break?" he asked on a Wednesday evening when Hope had been working steadily for three hours. She looked up from the box she was rummaging in, and Sean held out the glass of soda he'd poured for her. She had a folder in her hand, a streak of dust decorated her cheek, and wild tendrils of hair had escaped the ribbon with which she'd tied them back. Sean would have smiled at the picture she made, if it hadn't been for the despair in her eyes.

Instead, he walked farther into the room, a small frown crinkling his brow. "What's the matter, Hope? Having a problem?" He picked his way around the stacks of folders beside her and set the soda glasses on a little table within her reach.

She threw the folder back into the box with vicious force. "A problem? *A* problem?" She shoved herself to her feet, swiping her hair back from her face and leaving another smudge of dust on her forehead. "Yeah, I guess you could say I have a problem," she told him, her voice rising with stress. "I've been looking through these papers for weeks now, searching and sorting and looking, and..." She drew a deep, shaky breath, on the edge of tears. "I've looked and searched and hunted, and *I can't... find... anything!*"

Sean had her in his arms before the tears began to fall. She pressed her face into his shoulder, twining her arms around his waist and clinging tightly as her shoulders shook with sobs.

Sean stroked her back, murmured soothing nonsense and ached for her. She was letting this wild goose chase of hers tear her apart, and he didn't know how to help her. Warnings were no good. He'd already told her she was, at best, looking for a very small needle in a very big haystack, or at worst, looking for something that simply didn't exist. She'd ignored his warnings and pleaded with him to let her search anyway.

So he'd let her. What could it hurt? he'd thought, never imagining it would hurt her so much that he'd have to watch her coming apart in front of his eyes. And he simply couldn't stand to see her cry.

The storm was intense, but it didn't last long. Hope mastered herself as quickly as she could, pushing out of Sean's arms and twisting away from him, her face averted as she sniffed hard.

"Hope?" He stayed close but didn't reach to pull her into his arms again.

"I'm okay," she muttered, scrubbing the tears roughly off her face. "I'm fine."

She picked up her glass of soda, took a gulp and coughed as it went down the wrong way. She held up a hand when Sean moved to thump her on the back. "I'm okay," she insisted, her voice squeaky and thin.

"You don't sound okay."

She coughed again and cleared her throat. "I am. Really." Her voice was much stronger. "I'm fine, and I have to get back to work." She plopped down by the box and took another folder out, flipping it open and stared at the top page inside.

"No. You don't." Sean plucked the folder out of her hands and snapped it closed, tapping it against his chin as he looked down at Hope. "You don't need to work anymore tonight. You're so tired your eyes are crossing. Ah-ah-ah!" He caught her wrist when she tried to reach into the box again.

"Sean, let go!"

He didn't let go. "Come on." He hauled her to her feet, despite her resistance. She jerked against his grip on her wrist.

"Let go of me!"

"No." He pulled her across to the doorway, switched off the lights and urged her out into the hallway. "You're coming with me, and you're not working anymore tonight, you got that?"

"With you dragging me around by the hair like a caveman, I could hardly miss it, could I?" She glared at Sean as he slammed the door on Whitey's office and on her chances of working anymore that evening.

"I just want to make sure you've gotten the message." Sean headed down the hall, Hope in mutinous tow.

"I'm well aware that I'm being strong-armed, if that's what you mean," she snapped. "Are you going to throw me out and start refusing my phone calls again?"

"Maybe."

"What?" She jerked to a halt. Sean kept going, nearly yanking her off her feet before she stumbled a couple of steps and caught up with him.

"Maybe I will throw you out again if you don't stop making Whitey's avalanche of papers the be-all and end-all of your existence."

"I'm not doing that!"

"Oh, yeah?" He pushed her ahead of him through the living room doorway and let go of her wrist at last.

"Yes!" Hope spun around to face him, hands on hips, chin set at a pugnacious angle. "I'm not doing that. I'm working for my father's sake. To get—"

"To get him the credit he deserves," Sean finished for her in a singsong. "I know. I've heard it before, and I admire you for it, I honestly do. That's not the problem."

"Then why did you drag me out that way? I was busy."

"You're always busy. That's the problem. Lately, I don't think you'd eat or sleep if I didn't order in pizza and send you home at ten o'clock. You'd probably quit your teaching job to do this if you could afford to, and that's not healthy. That's an obsession."

"It's not an obsession, Sean. You're exaggerating. If I'm working hard, it's because I'm working for my father's name, and there's nothing wrong with that. A little hard work never hurt anybody."

"A little hard work sends people to the shrink with burnout," he muttered darkly.

"But think," she added with a smile that was just a bit too innocent, "the harder I work, the sooner I'll be finished, right?"

"Not necessarily, and if you think I'm going to fall for a ploy like that, you're mistaken." Sean's skepticism showed, and she flushed and looked away.

"Hope." He waited until she looked up again. "I know how much this means to you, but your involvement with it is getting out of control. You're obsessed with it, and that's not healthy."

"Oh, come on," she protested. "Don't be overdramatic. I have a job to do, and I want to do it. What's the big deal?"

"What if the job isn't doable?"

"What are you talking about?"

"You're working yourself to death on this quest of yours, but what if you can never finish it? You're searching for a 'truth' that may be no more than a figment of your ailing father's imagination. Frankly, I'm afraid of what will happen to you if that's all it turns out to be."

"That's *not* all it is!"

Sean reached out to take her hands, but Hope quickly stepped back. He let his hands fall to his sides. "Give yourself a break, Hope. I know what you want to do, what you intend to do, but don't ruin your health over it."

"My health is fine!"

"Except for the fatigue and the short temper and the depression because you've spent so much time looking and you haven't found anything yet." Sean blew his breath out in a hiss of frustration, worry and annoyance at her obstinacy. "Think about it, Hope." He reached out again, caught her hands in his this time, despite her token resistance. "You can't, or won't, rest until you've completed this quest of yours, right?"

"That's exactly right, so you might as well realize that it's futile to try to stop me!"

"But what then?"

"What do you mean, what then? Then I'll have done what I set out to do."

"Mmm-hmm. And what happens then? After you accomplish this all-important mission of yours, assuming you do, will you even have a life of your own to live?"

Hope squeezed his hands and smiled, seeking to reassure. "It's sweet of you to worry, Sean, but it's not necessary, really it's not. I'm fine."

He searched her face, unconvinced. "I hope you're right," he said at last. "I honestly hope you are, and I hope when this is over that you still have something to live for."

Hope left Sean's house knowing she hadn't convinced him of anything. It was too bad Sean was worried, but he just didn't understand. She'd have plenty of time to worry about the future when this was all over.

Right now all she could concentrate on was reaching her goal, because she had to do this.

She *had* to.

"Sean?" Don Molinari snapped his fingers under Sean's nose. "Sean? Anybody home in there?"

"Huh?" Sean came out of his reverie and frowned at his literary agent and friend. "What do you want?"

"Are you going to eat those shrimp, or do you just intend to give them an outing and then let the waiter take them back to the kitchen?"

"Oh." Sean looked down at his untouched lunch. "I guess I'm not very hungry. You want some?"

"If you insist." Don forked up one of the shrimp in garlic butter and ate it with gusto. "Those are great," he told Sean, going for another. "You don't know what you're missing."

"Cholesterol and bad breath." Sean passed the plate over. "Enjoy."

"Thanks." Don munched happily for a few minutes. "So. You gonna tell me what's wrong, or do I have to torture it out of you?"

Sean gave a humorless snort of laughter. "What kind of torture did you have in mind? Rack? Thumbscrews?"

"Torture by secretary," Don replied with the air of one who has all four aces up his sleeve. "Tell me, or I'll give Iris the go-ahead to harass you mercilessly by phone."

"Not that!" Sean threw up his hands in mock horror. "Anything but that!"

Iris was about fifty, with a raspy voice and a bull-dog's tenacity. She was undeterred by answering machines, answering services or unanswered phones, and she always got her man.

"So tell me." Don munched a shrimp and waited for his answer.

Sean knew perfectly well he couldn't outlast Iris. He could answer now or suffer later and answer in the end. He might as well answer now.

"It's Hope."

"The girl who's sorting Whitey's papers?" Don waited. "What about her?"

Sean sighed heavily. "I'm worried about her."

"Worried?" Don frowned. "Is that all? I expected you to say you're in love with her!"

Sean's jaw dropped. "In *what?*"

"In love with her," Don repeated, grinning. "You are, aren't you?"

"You're out of your mind!"

Don's grin widened. "You're worried about her. That's great."

"Why the hell is it great?"

"Because I didn't think I'd ever see you care enough about a woman to worry about her. I think that's great."

"Thanks a million, Don," Sean growled sarcastically. "You're a real pal."

"Your best buddy, Sean, with your best interests at heart. You care about the girl, you're worried to death about her. You undoubtedly love her."

"Don, you're out of your—"

"And since you love her," Don rolled along, undeterred, "all you have to do now is marry her."

"Damn it, Don! Will you find another groove in the record?"

Since he'd gotten married, Don had taken to seeing marriage as both the greatest social institution ever devised and the solution to any and every problem. Sean didn't. He was happy for Don, but fending off these recurrent matchmaking efforts was getting old.

"All right, all right!" Don capitulated for the moment. "Back to the original problem. You're worried about Hope. Why?"

"I'm worried about her health."

"Her health?" Don asked.

Sean nodded.

"Physical, mental or emotional health?"

"All of them."

"My God, what's the matter with her? Is she sick?"

"Not yet, but . . ."

"She's not sick *yet?* Sean, you're not making sense."

"It's not a real logical problem. Look, Don, I never told you the whole story of how I met Hope."

"I thought you met her because you're working on the biography of your father. Which," added Don, switching to his "agent" mode, "I hope you're working on, because your editor is starting to ask when she's going to see something more. I'd like to send her a chapter or two as soon as you can get something put together."

"It's going to be a while on that," Sean warned him. "Whitey's filing system borders on being an insurmountable obstacle."

"But isn't Hope doing most of the sorting for you?"

"Yeah, she's sorting. But that's only part of the deal. That's not the whole story." He signaled the waiter for another cup of coffee, sat back comfortably in his chair and began. "Hope just knocked on my door one day. Said she had something to tell me about Whitey's work."

When he reached the end of his story, Sean drained his coffee and looked across the table at Don. "So that's why I'm worried about Hope."

Don blinked and shook his head. "Yeah. I can see that." He ran a hand through what was left of his hair. "Whew! That's some story, Sean." He leaned forward, elbows on the table, gaze fixed on Sean. "Do you believe it?"

Sean shrugged. "What's important is that Hope believes it. She believes every word of it, with every fiber of her being. She's obsessed with proving that *her* father wrote *my* father's screenplays, and she can't even entertain the thought that her father might have made the whole thing up."

"Did he?" Don asked. "Make it up, I mean."

"Beats the hell out of me." Sean shrugged. "I don't know anything about Philip Carruthers's career, and I don't know anything about Whitey's career that a thousand entertainment journalists don't also know. Whitey could have written every word himself with a quill pen, or he could have had a stable of ghostwriters, for all I know to the contrary."

"What do you think?"

Sean looked down at his coffee cup and considered that for several moments.

"I think Whitey Baker wrote his own work," Sean said to the dregs in the bottom of his cup. "I also think that he had some sort of relationship with Philip Carruthers that I never knew about. I think I have to see this through, just like Hope does."

He looked up at Don. "I have to know the truth."

* * *

You could always just marry her.

Sean shook his head as he drove home, smiling wryly. Don had shouted that last bit of advice as Sean got into his car, unable to let the idea die. Sean couldn't get angry about it. Don was still a newlywed, with the kind of marriage that Sean had wanted and failed to get. Or failed to create.

Whatever Margo's problems and failings, Sean couldn't lay the whole blame for their failed marriage on her shoulders. She hadn't given him what he needed from marriage, but neither had he given her what she needed. She'd told him so, repeatedly, in the weeks before she'd walked out of the marriage and straight to a lawyer.

He hadn't been able to make the marriage work. He'd failed. Sean knew quite well that he was no good at marriage. He wasn't in love with Hope Carruthers, and he wasn't going to fall in love with her, because if he did fall in love, he might forget all the hard truths he'd learned. He might even be stupid enough to let himself think for a second time that love really could conquer all.

Which it couldn't.

No, what he felt for Hope was friendship and humane concern for her health.

And maybe lust. He couldn't deny what he'd felt when he kissed her. Still less could he deny what he'd felt when he slipped his hand inside that schoolgirl-cotton camisole she wore to caress her breast. There had been something unexpectedly, powerfully erotic about the combination of prim cotton covering a full, sweet breast, about naiveté and passionate response. Even the memory had the power to arouse him.

And that disturbing power was what had led him to send her away, to ignore her messages on his answering machine, to refuse to contact her. He'd tried to keep her away because he was just plain afraid to face her again.

That was one for the books. Sean Boudreaux, scared to face about a hundred and three pounds of little-brown-wren, convent-schooled virgin. Of course, he grinned to himself, this particular convent-schooled wren had the courage of a lion and the single-minded tenacity of a terrier.

She was an odd mix of timidity and nerve, shyness and courage, intriguing and exasperating at the same time.

Exasperating mostly because of her tunnel vision about this "quest" of hers. Sean's worry had been growing for a couple of weeks as he watched her become thinner, more stressed, more strung out. Her whole life was consumed with this task, and with each successive fruitless day, Hope grew grimmer and more fanatically determined to search more, search harder, until she found this proof she was so sure of.

Trouble was, Sean wasn't a bit sure the proof she'd staked so much of herself on even existed. He was more worried than he'd admitted to Don about what would happen to Hope if she never found what she was looking for. He wasn't sure she would be able to stand the physical strain of searching, and he was afraid she'd be emotionally shattered, destroyed, if the search turned out to be fruitless.

He turned into the canyon and negotiated the winding road automatically. He had to get her to let up, even for a little while. He couldn't convince her to stop working; he'd already tried that and failed.

But maybe, just maybe, he could get her mind off the work for a little while, even if it was just for an evening. All he needed was a plan.

By the time Sean turned up his drive, the plan was taking shape, and he was smiling.

He was waiting for Hope on the next Thursday afternoon, sitting by the open living room windows, listening for the sound of the BMW as it snarled its way up the drive. He had the door open before she could ring the bell.

"Hi, Hope." He stood blocking the doorway, hands braced on the frame.

"Hi, Sean." She looked at him, then looked past him into the hallway. "Can I come in?"

"Nope."

Chapter 8

Hope peered past him, into the house. "Nope?"

Sean fought a smile. "Nope."

"Well, umm . . ." She tipped her head to the side and studied him quizzically. "If you won't let me in, what are you going to do, then?"

"Not me, *we*," he corrected.

"Okay." Hope nodded. "What are *we* going to do?"

"*We* are not working tonight. We're going to a concert." Sean stepped out, pulled the door closed behind him and took her arm to lead her back down the steps to the BMW. "Come on. If we don't get moving, we're going to be late."

"Wait a minute!" Hope grabbed the side of the car before he could stuff her inside. "I'm not getting in here until you tell me where we're going!"

"I told you. A concert." He bent, hooked an arm behind her knees and scooped her neatly into the passenger seat. He clipped the safety belt across her and

slammed the door before she could climb back out, then
hustled around to drop into the driver's seat.

"Sean!" She grabbed his hand on the ignition before he could turn the key. "This is kidnapping! And
I'm not going anywhere with you until you tell me
where we're going!"

"I already told you. A con—"

"A concert," she parroted. "I know. You said that.
But I don't believe you."

"You don't believe me?" With a look of mock hurt,
he removed her hand and turned the key. "Why not?"

"Because it doesn't make sense!" she protested as he
aimed the car down the steep drive. "We can't go to a
concert dressed like this."

"Depends on the concert, doesn't it?"

Sean glanced at her floral print pants and rose-
colored cotton sweater, than at his own navy twill slacks
and tan sport coat, which he wore over a pale blue polo
shirt.

"For the Grateful Dead, we're overdressed."

"And for the L.A. Philharmonic we're under-
dressed," Hope shot back. "So what kind of concert
can it be that we're dressed for?"

"You'll find out." Smiling to himself, he turned his
attention to the road. They rode in silence for a time.

"Sean?"

"Yeah?"

"It's not actually the Grateful Dead . . . is it?"

Sean gave a shout of laughter and pulled onto the
freeway. "No," he assured her. "It's not the Grateful
Dead."

"Then what—"

"Just be patient for a few minutes and you'll see."

Hope watched the signs and held her tongue, until

one sign in particular caught her eye. "The Hollywood Bowl?" She watched the sign as Sean signaled and took the exit ramp. She swung around to Sean, her eyes glowing. "I've never been here!"

"Good." He glanced at her face and nodded in satisfaction. "You'll enjoy it. It's pretty spectacular the first time."

"I feel a little guilty, though."

"What the hell for?" he demanded.

"I should be working on the papers. I was—"

"No, you shouldn't be working on the damned papers! You should be taking a break, and you're going to."

"But I was going to start on the first file cabinet tonight."

"No! You've got to take a break or you're going to go crazy." They slowed to stop-and-go in the traffic entering the amphitheater drive. Sean caught her hand and waited until she was looking at him. "Listen to me, Hope. You aren't going to feel guilty about this, because I'm not going to let you. You aren't going to think about any of it tonight, not that damned pile of papers or your father or my father or anything to do with either of them! Got it?" He glared at her until she nodded.

"Okay," she said slowly. "I won't feel guilty."

"And you won't think about any of it. Got that?"

"Yes, I've got it."

"Good."

That was all he said, but Hope could feel powerful emotion beneath Sean's calm facade as he showed a parking pass, left the car in a reserved parking area near the rear of the bandshell and led her toward the entrance. Hope accompanied him quietly until she saw the placard announcing the night's program.

"The philharmonic?" she said. "Sean, I can't wear pants and a sweater to the philharmonic!"

"Sure you can. This is the Bowl. The regular rules don't apply."

"Really?" Hope let him pull her up a long ramp and into the amphitheater. They started down an aisle through the boxes, following a woman wearing a full-length mink.

"Really. You can wear anything here, from a strapless designer gown to jeans and a sweatshirt." He grinned at her. "Except that you'd freeze in the gown. It gets cold here when the sun goes down."

"Does it?" The setting sun still slanted through the hills, gilding the top of the bandshell. "It's nice and warm right now."

"Not for long." Sean stopped at the sixth row of boxes. "We're here, this row."

"Here?" Hope looked up at the stage. "It's practically in the orchestra."

"Just about." He ushered her to the third box along the row and opened the little gate. "This is it."

"This?" Hope stopped in the gateway. "But, Sean, this is somebody's box." The little hinged table was already folded out, draped with a white cloth and set with two candles, plates, glasses and a wicker basket. There were cushions on two of the six chairs and a plaid blanket neatly folded on another. "Their stuff is here and everything."

"Not their stuff, our stuff." He ushered her through the gate and seated her on one of the cushioned chairs. "This is ours."

"But who put it here?"

"The caterers."

"Caterers do seat cushions and blankets?"

"And picnics." He sat down, unfolded a napkin on his lap and opened the basket. "Gourmet picnics."

A slow smile of delight broke over Hope's face as she looked around her, at the seats rolling up the hillside until they seemed almost to be lost in the distance, at the people all around them, talking, smiling, enjoying their own preconcert picnics, at the stage with its waiting chairs and music racks. She settled back in her seat, unfolded her own napkin and looked across the little table at Sean.

"Gourmet picnics?" she asked.

"That's right."

"What's in a gourmet picnic?"

"Well..." He rummaged in the basket. "This one's supposed to have hors d'oeuvres, cold fillet of beef, salad, rolls and some kind of dessert."

"All that for a picnic?" She peered over the edge of the basket at the napkin-wrapped bundles inside. "Good grief!"

"It's a gourmet picnic, remember. And it better be good or those caterers will hear from me."

It was good. In fact, it was delicious, from the crudités and pâté to the meltingly rich pastries and coffee.

"Want another of these whatchamacallits?" Sean offered the small tray of pastries.

Hope shook her head. "I couldn't."

"Don't you like them?"

"How can you even ask, after watching me eat three of them!" She laughed. "Of course I like them. They're absolutely wonderful whatchamacallits, but I'm stuffed. I couldn't eat another bite."

"Coffee?"

"Maybe half a cup." She held the cup while he poured from a thermos. "Whoa! That's plenty."

While they ate, the amphitheater had been filling with people, and now the boxes all around them were occupied. Night was falling, and the sounds of twittering birds and the breeze rustling the trees mingled with the rumble of many voices and the chop-chop-chop of a helicopter high overhead.

When they'd packed the picnic remains back into the basket, Hope settled comfortably in her chair and sipped her coffee, sighing happily.

"Penny for them," Sean said.

"Hmm?"

"Your thoughts. Penny for them." He held up a bright copper coin.

She smiled at him. "I was just thinking how lovely and special this all is. Any concert is nice, but this is something out of the ordinary."

"Mmm-hmm." He took her hand and dropped the penny in her palm. "It is, isn't it? If you read the reviews of concerts here, they always complain about the acoustics, about police sirens and the planes flying overhead. I think they're missing the point. The acoustics may not be perfect, and you hear the occasional airplane, but it's all part of the experience. A concert here isn't like a concert anywhere else."

"I can see that." Hope looked up at the sky darkening from rose-tinted navy to star-dotted indigo. "When will the concert start?" she wondered.

"Ten minutes or so. The musicians should be coming out anytime."

As he said the words, three cellists emerged onstage and took their seats, leaning over their instruments as they tuned them and loosened up, playing a few bars of a concerto. Hope straightened in her chair, watching and listening as the orchestra assembled. She was on the edge of her chair when the conductor strode onstage, and as the first notes sounded, she let herself be swept away into the music.

Sean didn't know which was better, listening to the concert or watching Hope's rapt enjoyment of it. He didn't think she even noticed the rapidly cooling night air, but when she started to shiver, he moved his chair close to hers and wrapped the plaid blanket around both of them.

Intermission brought her out of her trance.

"Wasn't that wonderful?" She shifted in her chair and noticed the blanket around her. "What's this?"

"You were shivering." He slid his arm around her shoulders, then tucked the soft wool back into place. "But you were so wrapped up in the music you didn't even notice."

She smiled, abashed. "Music does that to me."

"There's no reason to be embarrassed about it." Sean gave her shoulders a gentle shake. "Far better to honestly enjoy the music than to sit through it and pretend pseudosophisticated disdain."

Hope chuckled. "All right, but if I show signs of wanting to rush the stage when the flautist plays, hold me back, okay?"

"Deal. You don't pretend to be above it all, and I won't let you attack the little bald flautist."

"Thanks." She half turned within the circle of his arm and smiled up at him. "And thank you, Sean, for bringing me. This is like a dream. I'll never forget it."

"Good." He bent his head to brush a kiss across her lips, then straightened, looking up at the stage. "They're coming back."

If Hope felt a pang of disappointment, she wouldn't admit it to herself. She did snuggle just a little closer against Sean's side, though. For warmth, of course.

The first half of the program had been baroque music, cool, intellectual, somewhat challenging to the listener. The second half, however, was lushly romantic, full of fire and emotion.

Tears stood in Hope's eyes at the beauty of it, and when she felt Sean's fingertips beneath her chin, she turned her face eagerly up to his. The kiss began gently, almost uncertainly, but the passion in the music was also beating through them, and Hope's lips parted willingly under the slight pressure of his mouth, not so much allowing as asking him to deepen the kiss.

Beneath the folds of the blanket, he pulled her closer, a hand on her knee, then her waist, then drifting up to rest just below the swell of her breast. Hope felt her heart trip, then resume hammering in a quicker, harder beat, felt her breath catch for a moment, just before he covered her breast with his palm.

The breath shuddered out of her on a sigh, and she clutched Sean's shoulders beneath the blanket, forgetting for a mindless moment that they were at a concert, sitting in the middle of a crowd of several thousand people.

For a moment, just a moment, she thought she felt the same madness in Sean, the yielding to passion, the surrender of will, but then he stiffened. He drew away slowly, taking her hands from his shoulders, clasping them between his as he turned to face the stage again.

Hope tried to concentrate on the music, but the earlier trancelike absorption was gone. In its place was a different kind of magic, a crystalline awareness of Sean beside her, his thigh pressed to hers, his hands clasping hers, while the music, rich and romantic, surrounded them. If anything, it was a better kind of magic.

The concert ended eventually, though. The music stopped and the lights came up, and reality returned, pushing magic aside. Sean scarcely looked at her as he gathered up the basket and blanket to return to the catering office, scarcely touched her as they filed slowly out with the rest of the crowd. In the car he was silent, his face set, almost grim.

Hope stood it until they were on the freeway.

"Sean?"

He kept his eyes on the road ahead. "Mmm?"

"Is something wrong?"

"Nothing but this traffic." He swore under his breath and signaled to change lanes. "Listen, can we talk after I get off the freeway? It's really a mess tonight."

"Yes. Of course."

Hope subsided into her seat, her face turned away from Sean as she looked out the window. He glanced at the back of her head, then looked forward, his mouth set in a grim line.

He didn't want conversation tonight, not after that kiss back there in the box. He wanted—

Hell, he knew what he wanted, but that wasn't going to happen. He was going to take Hope home, convince her they could have this conversation another time, see her safely inside and leave.

But even after he'd done all those things, he couldn't stop thinking, about the evening, about Hope, about that kiss.

His intention had been to distract Hope from her work on the papers. He should have taken her to play miniature golf or something. He should have known better than to try to do it with a concert under the stars.

Just went to show, he thought with a grimace of self-rebuke, that jaded, cynical old Sean Boudreaux was as susceptible as the next man to a little romantic atmosphere. Okay, so it was a lot of romantic atmosphere, but still he should have kept his head. Should have kept his lips and his hands to himself, too! He should have done a lot of things that he hadn't done.

He wanted to turn around, drive back to Hope's house and take her in his arms and kiss her and make love to her all through the night. He wanted to keep driving as far and as fast as he could, away from the dangerous temptation of her passionate, untutored kisses and beautiful, virginal body. She infuriated him, she inflamed him, she terrified him.

He didn't want Hope, or any woman, getting under his skin, intruding into his thoughts. He didn't want to worry about whether she was working too hard, whether she was eating well or sleeping enough, or whether her old junker of a car was running okay. He didn't want to worry whether the kids in her second grade were running her ragged.

You only worried about people when they mattered to you. He didn't want Hope Carruthers to matter. The last time someone mattered to him, he'd walked blindly into a situation that closely approximated hell. He'd rather spend the rest of his days alone than walk back into that.

If he said any of this to Hope, of course, she'd talk about things like true love and forever and happy endings. Sean knew all too well that all that was nonsense, a fairy tale.

He knew what reality was between men and women, knew that forever didn't really last all that long. He'd grown up watching what "till death us do part" really

meant as his father married and remarried and married
yet again.

Whitey had married five times. *Five times!* He'd been
divorced five times, too, and in the end, he'd died alone.
So much for forever.

Sean had never asked his father why he kept marrying that way. He wondered how Whitey would have answered that question. He'd probably have said that this
time, each time, was the real thing, that this was love,
that this one was *the* one.... That this time was forever.

Whitey had undoubtedly been convinced each time
that that was true, yet each time it had ended in bitterness and acrimony.

Sean had thought those same things once, that this
was it, this was real and true and forever. He'd been
wrong, just like Whitey, and his "forever" had ended
in the kind of acrid bitterness that left scars on the soul.
Deep scars that hurt if they were touched, scars that
were a constant presence in the back of Sean's mind.

Whenever he looked at Hope Carruthers, when he
thought of making love with her, of caring for her, of
never wanting to let her out of his life, the thoughts were
like cruel fingers probing those scars, reawakening the
painful memories of bitterness and hurt and the acid,
corrosive hate that love could become.

Hope deserved someone who could at least start out
with a belief in forever, whether the belief survived in
the end or not. She needed someone who was still capable of optimism. Sean could no longer give her that.
His well of optimism had dried up years before. He had
nothing left to offer. There was no future for them, and
it would be stupid and cruel to let her imagine there
might be.

* * *

Hope was confused. Hope was hopelessly confused. Hope was hopeless. She wrapped her bathrobe more closely around her and walked back into her bedroom, laughing wanly at the bit of rather stupid wordplay. If she didn't laugh she'd cry, and she'd done too much of that already.

It had happened again, just like before. Sean kissed her, and she responded, and then he'd pushed her away, both physically and emotionally. He hadn't wanted to talk to her in the car coming home, had put off talking at all, and he hadn't been able to shove her through her front door and drive away fast enough.

And it hurt. Her brave smile faded. It hurt so badly, because she'd wanted that kiss, had wanted his arms around her. She'd wanted things that she didn't even know how to describe. She wanted things only Sean could satisfy, but Sean didn't want her.

"I could get really tired of having lunch meetings with a zombie, you know."

Sean and Don were back at The Patio for another business lunch. Don had ordered the shrimp in garlic butter this time, while Sean was pushing a crab enchilada with black beans around with his fork, making a mess on his plate without eating anything.

Don watched him for a moment, then reached out and took the fork from his hand. "Sean!"

"What?" Sean finally looked up and grabbed his fork back. "Give me that! I'm eating!"

"No you're not, you're making mudpies out of that thing. It's not a pretty sight, either." Don shook his head and ate another shrimp.

Sean sighed and laid his fork down. "I hate it when you're right, Don."

"You hate it when I'm nosy, too, but I'm still gonna ask. What's got you so distracted that you can't even pay attention when your literary agent is talking?" He grinned. "Or do I even need to ask?"

Sean scowled. "Yes, it's Hope, if that's what you're getting at."

"Of course it's Hope. But what is it about Hope that has you so distracted this time? Are you still worried that she's working too hard?"

"She is working too hard, but that's not what I'm worried about."

"What, then? You worried about how to propose to her? Try a fancy restaurant with a strolling violinist. That's where I proposed to Susie, and she loved it. She wants to go back there on our first anniversary."

"I'm glad you made Susie happy, Don, but that's not—"

"On one knee, then. They love it when you go down on one knee and pull a ring out of your pocket."

"Don, will you give it a rest? I'm not proposing to Hope!"

"Why not? You worry about her all the time. You might as well be married. Then you'd have a right to take care of her."

"I'm not talking about marriage, damn it!"

"Why not? Marriage is great. You ought to try it sometime."

"I did try it, remember?" Sean said coldly. "And if that was great, I hope to God I never have to deal with bad."

"I know you had a bad marriage, Sean, and I'm sorry. But that doesn't mean you can't give it another chance."

"In my case it does. Don, will you just listen to me for a minute?" This time Sean took Don's fork away. "Just shut up about marriage and listen?"

"I'll listen. You don't have to take my silverware away."

"To get you to stop chomping on those shrimp, I do."

Don looked at Sean's face and sobered. He took his fork back and laid it beside his plate. "I'm listening. What's the problem?"

"Hope is working too hard, but that's just the symptom of the problem. She's so wrapped up in this search of hers that it scares me. She's totally convinced that her father actually wrote a bunch of Whitey's screenplays. I don't know what it's going to do to her if she can't find the proof she wants."

"You don't think she'll find that proof, do you?"

Sean rubbed a hand over his face tiredly. "No. Not really. Whitey and I didn't get along, but he *was* my father. We did talk about things, once in a while, anyway, but I never heard him mention Philip Carruthers. As far as I know, he never even knew the man, but—"

"But what? Are you saying you actually believe this story of hers?"

Sean shook his head, but slowly, as if less certain than he'd once been. "It doesn't make any sense. But I'm not sure I actually disbelieve it, if you know what I mean. She's so convinced, so sure, that I can't completely discount what she believes."

After a moment's consideration, Don nodded. "I can see what you mean. But how do you prove it, one way or the other?"

"By going through his papers, just as Hope's been doing. The trouble is, even if there is something, I don't think she's going to find it in his office."

"No?"

"No. If Whitey really did have a secret this big to keep, he wouldn't have left records of it lying around. Especially not in his office."

"Why wouldn't he put them in his office?"

"Because it wasn't the least bit private. He had a secretary and a personal assistant who worked in there all the time, and he was always sending people in there to look for this or that piece of paper. He couldn't have concealed anything in there, because most days half the universe seemed to be rummaging around in there."

"Makes sense," Don agreed. "He wouldn't have hidden something important in his office, so the question becomes where he would have hidden it."

"Bingo. And I've thought of someplace where he just might have done that, but I don't know whether to tell Hope about it or not."

"Why on earth wouldn't you tell her? You're already letting her sort through his papers, so what difference could it make?"

"It could make a difference to her. She's got herself on an emotional roller coaster, and it's getting to her. It seems like she's either euphoric or depressed these days, and I don't want to be responsible for raising any more false hopes."

"On the other hand," Don said, "if there's a chance that you do know a place where Whitey might have hidden secrets, don't you owe it to Hope to let her be in

on the discovery? After all, you'd never have looked for
secret papers if she hadn't come to you with this story,
would you?"

"Of course not."

"And if there is something to find, whether it's what
Hope is expecting or not, it will make your biography
that much better, won't it?"

"New Secrets Revealed?" Sean almost grinned.
"Sounds like a headline in a tabloid."

"But speaking as your literary agent, I have to think
of the value to the book . . ."

"If it's something that's even worth including in the
book."

"Hope, then. Think about her. Doesn't Hope have
the right to be in on even the possibility of a discovery
like that?"

Chapter 9

Didn't Hope have a right to know what he was thinking of?

Didn't Hope have a right to be in on the search?

Would he feel worse if he told Hope what he'd thought of and they found nothing, or if he didn't tell her and actually found something?

The answer was there, waiting for him to accept it.

He'd lunched with Don on Monday, and by Wednesday he knew what he would do. He waited until they'd finished eating the carryout Chinese he'd insisted on feeding her.

"Hope?"

"Yes?" She paused on her way out of the kitchen, but she didn't look at him.

She hadn't been looking at him very much lately. She didn't smile into his face anymore or even meet his eyes, if there was any way to avoid it. Sean told himself it was better that way, but it didn't feel better.

With a silent sigh, he set the dishes he carried in the sink and wiped his hands on a towel.

"There's something I need to tell you."

"What is it?" Rather than look at him, she studied a dried-flower arrangement in a bowl on the kitchen island.

"I've thought of—" He scowled at her bent head. "Hope, could you look at me, please?"

She hesitated, then turned slowly, lifting her head to look across the room at him. Her eyes, those gorgeous green eyes that could flash with fire and passion, were distant, hiding her feelings.

"All right," she said coolly. "I'm looking at you. What is it?"

"It's Whitey's records." He wished she'd smile, just a little, or come a step closer. He'd find it easier to talk to her if she wasn't so obviously wary of him.

"What about them?"

"You haven't found anything in his office."

"No. I haven't."

"I was thinking about that, and I realized something."

"That I'm not going to find anything?"

"No." He shook his head and moved a step closer to her. "When you asked to look through his office and I said yes, I figured it couldn't hurt, because after all, there wasn't anything to find."

"Because you didn't believe me."

He shrugged. "There was no real reason why I should, you know."

This time it was Hope who conceded the point. She nodded, once. "I know."

"Anyway, I figured you'd sort through those papers until you got tired of it, give up, and that would be that." He half smiled, crossing the rest of the distance between them. "But you surprised me."

"By what?" she asked bitterly. "It can't be because I haven't found a thing. You predicted that."

"By the fact that you stuck with it. By the fact that you really do believe your story is true. By the fact that you're not giving up. Your persistence has made me think."

"That I'm certifiably nuts, right?"

He shook his head and reached for her hand. To his surprise, she didn't jerk away.

"I think that maybe—just maybe—I was too quick to dismiss what you told me."

"Do you believe me?" she asked. Her hand, which had been lying limp in his, tensed, her fingers pressing his.

Sean shook his head. "I still don't have any reason to believe it's true, but I don't feel like I should be so quick to dismiss the idea out of hand."

"Well, gee golly wow." Hope pulled her hand away. "Will you alert the press, or shall I?"

"Don't be sarcastic." Sean followed as she wandered across the kitchen to look out the window, her back to him. "When I started to think about it a little more open-mindedly, when I began to look at things differently, I realized something."

There was a moment of silence, then Hope sighed in exasperation. "Okay, I'll bite. What did you realize?"

"I realized that you aren't going to uncover any secrets in the papers that are here in Whitey's office."

"Another news flash!" Hope spun on her heel, throwing up her hands in mock amazement. "Since I've searched more than half the stuff in there and found

absolutely nothing, I can't understand how you figured that out."

"Will you quit with the sarcasm?" Sean caught her
hand and pulled her around to face him. "I realized
something, once I started looking at your story as a
possibility, however remote."

"What did you—"

"I realized," he went on as if she hadn't spoken,
"that if Whitey actually did have secret records—and
I'm only saying *if* he did—then he wouldn't have kept
them there in his office, where anyone could find them.
He may have been a lot of things, but he wasn't stupid."

"So I've been plowing through those mountains of
papers for nothing?"

"I wouldn't have put it that bluntly, but yes."

"So *if* he had secret records, he wouldn't have kept
them in his office?"

"Mmm-hmm." Sean shook his head. "He would
have hidden them, and I may have an idea where."

"You do?" Hope couldn't keep the eagerness out of
her voice, and she gripped his hand unconsciously.

Sean held her hand, kept his voice level and tried to
bring her excitement down to a more reasonable level.
"Don't get your hopes up. I don't *know* that there's
even anything to hide," he said. "But if there was, I've
thought of a place where he might have hidden things
he wanted to keep secret."

He fell silent for a breathless moment. Hope gripped
his hand tighter, shaking it a little as she bounced on her
toes, unable to contain the excitement bubbling up in
her.

"Come on, Sean. Don't drag out the suspense! What
is this place? Where is it?"

"Santa Barbara."

"The town of Santa Barbara?"

"That's the one," he told her. "Up the coast, pretty scenery, old mission, outrageous real estate prices?"

"That's the one," she agreed. "Are you saying we have to search the entire town of Santa Barbara?"

"We don't even have to sift all the sand on the beach," he told her. "Whitey had a house in Santa Barbara."

"He did?"

"Yep. He had it for as long as I can remember. Since before I can remember, actually. Whitey and I spent a few weekends there when I was a kid. The last time I was there was right before our big fight. I never went back, but I know he didn't sell the house. It was listed as part of the estate when the will was probated."

"You didn't go to see it when you inherited it?" she wondered.

Sean shook her head, short and sharp. "I never wanted to."

"I see." And she did see. She saw more, perhaps, than he wanted her to. "But you didn't sell the house?"

He shook his head again. "It was being taken care of. There was no hurry to do anything about it."

"And now?"

"Now I think it's a good thing I didn't sell that house. Because if Whitey was going to hide papers, I think the Santa Barbara house is one of the more logical places for him to have done it."

"You really do?" She tried to speak calmly but couldn't keep the eagerness out of her voice.

"I do," he said, "*if* he actually had any secret records and *if* he wanted a place to hide them. Look, Hope—" he placed his hands warningly on her shoulders ''—I don't want you to get your hopes up. This is nothing but a wild guess, and the odds are it won't pay off.''

"How can you say that?" she demanded, pulling free and spinning across the room on the bubble of excited anticipation she could no longer suppress. "This makes such a difference! Now it all makes sense. This is why I looked and looked without finding anything. I couldn't find anything, because it's not here! It was never here, because why would he keep secret things where just anybody could find them?''

She spun to a stop and whirled around to address Sean. "When can we go to Santa Barbara to look? Can we go tonight?''

"It's too late. It'd be midnight by the time we got there, and you have to work tomorrow.''

"Tomorrow night, then? We could leave as soon as I'm done with school.''

He shook his head. "We'd still have a time problem. Look, Hope, I don't want you to get carried away with this. It's just a guess, and probably wrong at that.''

"Of course it's not wrong! Don't be such a wet blanket, Sean. You know you're a genius! This is a brilliant idea. It's so brilliant it has to be right!''

"Hope, stop it!" he almost shouted. He grabbed her hands, forcing them down to her sides. "Listen to me. Please.'' He waited until she was looking at him.

"I don't want you to get carried away like this. I'd never have brought it up if I'd thought you couldn't handle it. This is just a guess, nothing more. It may lead to nothing. In fact, it'll *probably* lead to nothing. If we go up there and search, odds are we won't find any more than we've found here, so I don't want you getting excited about it. That's setting yourself up for a fall.''

''I see.'' The excitement faded from Hope's face, to be replaced by irritation. ''And you think I can't handle it if we don't find anything?''

''I think you can handle a very great deal. It's just—''

''Come off it, Sean. You think I'm going to break into pieces if some little thing goes wrong. Admit it.''

''I worry about you. What's wrong with that?''

''Nothing's wrong with it, as long as you don't get carried away with it. You can't stop me from feeling hope and anticipation, so you might as well not try. If I want to be excited, I will be.''

''And what about when you're disappointed? What then?''

''Then I'll deal with it,'' she retorted. ''Now quit worrying about things that you don't need to worry about and tell me when we can go.''

He sighed, his mouth thinning to a grim line. There was no point in arguing with her; it was obvious he wasn't going to change her mind.

''How about Friday?'' he said reluctantly. ''We can leave as soon as you're finished at school and have the whole weekend to search.''

''Not until Friday?'' Her face fell in dismay. ''Do we have to wait that long?''

''Oh, come on, Hope, it's two measly days! I know you're impatient, but surely you can wait that long.''

Hope glowered at him, mutinous. ''Only if I have to.''

''Don't get your hopes up too high. You'll only be disappointed if nothing turns up.''

Hope sighed in exasperation. It was Friday noon and she was too excited about the upcoming trip to Santa Barbara to be interested in hearing words of caution.

"Margaret, you sound just like Sean."

"Is that so bad?" Sister Margaret blew a quick blast on her whistle and waved a group of boys away from the street.

"Maybe. He's come up with what sounds like a very good possibility, and all he can say is, 'Don't get your hopes up, don't get your hopes up.' This is the best lead we've had to Whitey's secret papers. Why *shouldn't* I get my hopes up, for Pete's sake?"

"Because as I understand it, there may not be any secret papers, Hope. Shouldn't you keep that in mind?"

Hope rolled her eyes. "With you and Sean around, how can I forget? Don't you see, though? I have to believe there are some records, somewhere, to prove what I know. I have to believe that!"

Margaret frowned. "I understand how you feel, Hope, but be careful. Don't let what you want to believe blind you to reality."

After a moment, Hope nodded. "All right, but I want you to know, and I'm telling Sean, too, that I won't let that so-called 'reality' blind me to hope."

"So you and Margaret can be as pessimistic as you want, Sean. I'm going to believe it's there until I'm proven wrong." Hope slid into the passenger seat of his car and fastened the seat belt.

Sean walked around the car, got in and fastened his own belt, then paused with his hand on the ignition key. "Who are you trying to convince, Hope? Me—or yourself?"

So that was the kind of mood Sean was in, was it? Well, Hope wasn't about to let him dampen her enthusiasm, and she was feeling just belligerent enough not to care what he thought of it. And anyway, all the cautionary words in the world couldn't dim the fever of her enthusiasm.

She knew, she just *knew*, that they would find something at the house in Santa Barbara, some sort of records or evidence that would prove her father's authorship of those screenplays. She knew, and nothing Margaret said, nothing Sean said, could persuade her otherwise.

Hugging her certainty to herself, Hope looked out the window at the passing scenery and tried to ignore Sean and his cautions.

It almost worked.

It might have worked, except she cared about Sean, and she cared what he thought. She didn't want him to think she was hopelessly naive or a fool with tunnel vision, unable to acknowledge more than one side of an issue. She even understood Sean's reservations. In his position, she probably wouldn't believe it, either.

She had the advantage of knowing the truth, though. She'd listened to her father talk about his career, about his friendship with Whitey Baker, and the strange and wonderful turn that friendship took when Philip's world began to fall to pieces around him.

She'd been there, but Sean hadn't. He hadn't seen the passion in her father's aging face, or the gleam of life in his fading eyes when he talked about events of thirty years before, but she had. She had the advantage over Sean, for she knew the truth. She believed everything her father had told her, and she had to believe that she would, eventually, be able to prove that truth. If she let that belief slip, if she let doubt in, she would be letting her father down, and she wouldn't, couldn't, do that.

If she could only find a way to make Sean understand that she wasn't just chasing a pipe dream, maybe he would stop worrying about her. And if he could stop worrying so much, maybe he could work with her instead of spending all his time cautioning her against being obsessive about something she considered she had every right to be obsessive about.

And maybe, just maybe, she and Sean wouldn't be at odds with each other anymore. Hope leaned her head against the window and sighed, watching the dark mountains slide past.

Sean glanced over at Hope when she sighed, and saw that she was leaning against the window, looking outside, her eyes soft, her expression sad.

Why did she look sad? Before they left, she'd been bubbling with excitement, eagerly anticipating the search to come. He turned back to the road, frowning.

He'd have thought he'd be glad to see her overeagerness moderated, but he didn't want to see her sad. He just wanted this mess over with!

Right or wrong, good or bad, once it was over, they'd know what they had to deal with. He was no longer absolutely convinced that Hope was wrong about her father and the screenplays, but he was a hell of a long way from being certain she was right. The odds were against it, but he had just enough doubts to be willing to continue the search.

He might have changed his mind to that extent, but he still thought Hope was setting herself up for a fall. That was his biggest worry. Would she be able to handle the disappointment that he still felt was inevitable?

She'd invested so much of her life, of herself, in this quixotic search that she couldn't even allow herself to think about failure. If she failed, *when* she failed, would she be able to handle it?

He was afraid she was in emotional trouble, and that scared him. How could he help? What could he do, when the woman in emotional trouble was far too close to him for any kind of objectivity and distance? How could he protect her without getting so close to her that he'd hurt her in spite of himself?

His hands clenched the wheel until his knuckles whitened.

She was too good for him. She was too good. She loved kids; she taught school; she was determined to honor her father's memory. She was idealistic, intelligent, well educated, not to mention sweet, passionate and beautiful . . . and a virgin. Hell, she was perfect!

And he, who had no illusions about his current and past state of imperfection, was trying to protect her. That was some kind of joke, wasn't it? If she needed protecting from anything or anyone in this world, it was somebody like cynical, jaded, bitter old Sean Boudreaux. "Damn!" he muttered.

He wasn't aware he had spoken aloud until Hope looked over at him. "Sean?"

"Huh?"

"Is something wrong?"

He glanced at her. "No, nothing's wrong," he said curtly, and looked away again.

He drove for perhaps another five minutes, while the first spatters of rain hit the windshield, gradually becoming heavier. Up ahead, lightning flashed dramatically over the mountains.

"Sean?" Hope broke the silence again, her tone uncertain.

"What?"

"Have I done something, or said something, to make you angry?"

"No."

She bit her lip, then forged on despite his surly tone. "Sean, I can tell something's wrong. If it's something I—"

"It's not!" he snapped. "You didn't do anything, okay?"

"But maybe I can hel—"

"No!" He glanced over, and wished he hadn't. The hurt in her eyes was like a punch in the stomach, but the alternative was to tell her the truth. He jerked around to stare out the windshield again. "No," he repeated more quietly. "There's nothing wrong. I was just thinking. There's nothing you've done wrong. It's just that the rain's getting bad. The road's a little slick."

"Oh." Her voice was very small. "Okay."

She subsided into her seat, her face averted once again, and Sean felt like a heel for pushing her away. The only thing that could be worse than hurting her feelings this way would be letting her get close, the way he wanted to. In the long run, that would inflict a hurt far more serious.

She probably thought she was in love with him. In fact, looking back over events of the last few weeks, Sean was pretty sure she did. And if she did, he had to keep pushing her away until she gave up on him and the dead end he would be for her. She wanted somebody to love, somebody to marry.

A woman like her had a right to expect marriage. She deserved it all, love, commitment and marriage. She deserved better than a cynical, burnt-out case like him.

Once upon a time he could have offered her what she deserved, but no longer. He couldn't promise love or a lifetime or happiness, because he knew how easily those promises could be turned to discontent and betrayal. He glanced at Hope's averted face. Her feelings might be hurt now, but better that than a far greater hurt later on.

He couldn't give her what she might think she wanted, but at least he could help her to reach the end of this quest of hers. If his guess did turn out to be right and Whitey had hidden some papers in the Santa Barbara house, then Sean was prepared to tear the house apart brick by brick and board by board until he found them.

When he finally pulled to a stop in front of the house, though, he just sat in the car, looking at it.

Hope had recovered her sense of humor.

"Sean?"

"Hmm?"

"I hate to keep repeating myself, but is something wrong?"

"No." He shook his head. "I'm just looking."

"At the house? This is the right house, isn't it?"

"Yeah. This is the house." He smiled into the darkness.

"Then, you should forgive me for asking, but why aren't we getting out of the car?"

Sean heard the smile in her voice. Apparently she'd decided to forgive him for his surliness. He was glad, more than he'd have thought he could be. He reached out to touch her hand lightly.

"It's weird, you know."

"What's weird?"

"The way places you remember from childhood look the same, but different, when you see them again."

"I know what you mean."

"Take this house. I haven't seen it in maybe twenty years. It's the same house, but it looks smaller, like it's shrunk, somehow."

"Or is it just that the bushes are bigger?" Shrubs that must have been foundation plantings thirty years before masked the windows and reached the eaves.

"I get bills from a gardening service. They're supposed to be taking care of pruning and things like that."

"Maybe you should change gardeners." Hope regarded the yard dubiously. In the driving rain and fast-fading light, it was a miniature jungle.

"Maybe. I wonder how the cleaning service has done with the inside."

"One way to find out." Hope put her hand on the door handle. "Go in and see."

"Yeah." Sean took the door handle and pushed, then paused. "You know, it's stupid, but now that we're here, I don't really..." His smile was strained. "I don't really want to go in."

"That's not stupid," Hope said quietly. "It would be strange if you didn't feel a little funny about being here after all these years. You aren't alone, though."

Sean looked over at her and his teeth flashed in a sudden grin. "Will you protect me from spiders and boogeymen and stuff like that?"

Hope grinned back. "Sure. But if we run into any slugs, you're on your own."

"Slugs aren't your favorite critters?"

"Yech! Like snails without shells! And I'm not crazy about snails, either." Hope opened her door. "Come on, Sean. It's time to go in."

They ran through the downpour to the small covered porch and huddled there while rain drummed on the leaves of the overgrown shrubs on either side. Sean unlocked the bolt, then turned the knob and swung the door inward. It opened easily onto a thick, musty darkness.

Sean didn't move, and after a moment, Hope touched his hand.

"Sean?"

"Yeah?"

"It's time to go in."

"Yeah." He turned his wrist to clasp her hand in his and walked inside.

Chapter 10

The house was chilly inside, the air stale and still, too long undisturbed. Hope followed as Sean felt his way inside, running his fingers over the wall in search of a light switch.

He flipped it up, lights blazed on, and an ear-piercing siren shrieked from somewhere all too close.

Blinded by the glare, deafened by the noise, Hope covered her ears and cringed against the wall as Sean searched rapidly around the doorways that opened off the entry hall. His lips were moving steadily, and though Hope couldn't hear what he was saying, it looked like swearing to her.

"*. . . damned burglar alarm!*"

In the sudden silence, his words were unnaturally loud. He stopped and looked sheepishly at Hope.

"Sorry. I forgot about the alarm. I'm only glad I remembered the code the lawyers told me."

Hope's ears were still ringing. "If you forgot about the alarm, how could you remember the code?"

"Whitey picked numbers he could remember."

She waited for a moment. "Don't leave me hanging, Sean. What are they?"

He started to smile. "One two three four five six."

Hope's lips twitched. "I'm glad he picked something the burglars will have a hard time figuring out."

Sean was fighting a smile of his own. "He was cagey that way." He turned away toward the living room, then glanced back. "I bet he wrote it down and kept it in his wallet, though, just in case."

Hope gave a hoot of laughter, and Sean caught her hand to pull her along with him. "Come on, Hope, let's see what kind of shape this place is in."

The entry had been furnished with a worn oriental rug and a half-round Chippendale table. The mate to that table stood just inside the living room, and a larger version of the rug covered most of the floor. There was a sofa before the fireplace, flanked by two chairs and occasional tables, with a coffee table made of driftwood in front of it. The furnishings were pretty ordinary, if shabby. It was the shelves that were unusual.

Bookshelves and cupboards in all styles were ranged around the walls, filling every inch of space and only grudgingly leaving room for windows, doors and fireplace. Hope turned in a full circle and saw that there were even books above the windows, stacked on boards that formed bridges from the top of one bookcase to the top of another. The only wall space in the entire room that was free of storage was the massive stone chimneypiece that rose from the fireplace to the ceiling. That had a clutter of pictures and certificates hung on it, while the mantel was thick with bric-a-brac.

She stopped and looked closer. That wasn't just any old bric-a-brac up there. Amid the clutter of figurines, paperweights and ashtrays, there was an Emmy, and down at the other end, half-hidden behind an ugly "Souvenir of San Francisco" vase, was—

"An Oscar?" she breathed.

Across the room, Sean let the curtains fall back over the window. "Yeah." He glanced at the mantel. "I only found two of them at the house in L.A."

"Didn't you wonder where the other one was?" Hope touched the little statuette lightly, almost reverently, with a fingertip. It was dusty.

"It was either around or it wasn't," Sean replied. "For all I knew, one of the wives had it, or he gave it to somebody. It didn't really matter."

Hope opened her mouth, looked at Sean and closed it again. What could you say to a man who thought his father's Academy Award didn't matter? She touched the Oscar one more time, then turned away.

Sean was walking slowly around the room, surveying the ceiling-high shelves and the cupboards that were below some of them, all stuffed beyond capacity. He looked over his shoulder at Hope.

"Remind you of anything?"

"Like his study in L.A.?" She looked at the overflowing shelves and crammed cupboards. "He didn't believe in throwing anything away, did he?"

"A confirmed pack rat." Sean shook his head, then, suddenly brisk, strode back toward the entry hall. "Well, now we know what kind of search we're dealing with, so let's check out the rest of this place."

"The rest" was an old-fashioned kitchen, big enough to accommodate a large table and eight chairs with ease, one good-sized bedroom and two smaller ones, and a big bathroom, complete with clawfoot tub. There was a half basement, unusual for California, and an attic that Sean refused to explore until morning and daylight. The whole house was clean enough, but the rooms had a slightly down-at-heels air, the once-good furnishings and appointments now worn and forlorn.

Sean turned on the furnace, checked the water heater and got out sheets and towels, while Hope put away the groceries they'd brought, found a pot and made coffee. They met in the living room after about an hour of chores. Hope curled up on the sofa with her cup of coffee and Sean lounged on the edge of the raised hearth, beside the fire he'd built. The storm still raged outside, a gale off the Pacific howling over the roof and hurling rain against the windows, but inside it was growing cozy, with the smell of coffee, the fire crackling cheerfully and Whitey's clutter all around them.

"How does it feel?"

Sean had been studying the fire, but he looked around when Hope spoke. "How does what feel?"

"Being in this house again."

"Weird." He shifted his shoulders as if he felt someone behind him. "Even more than at the house in L.A., I feel as if Whitey is here. I have the feeling he's going to walk out of the kitchen any minute, carrying a cup of cocoa and muttering about how badly the latest script is going. Everything's the same, yet it's different. I remembered this place as new, bright and cheerful, not faded and shabby."

"Time changes things," she reminded him gently. "It's inevitable."

"I know. The memories are stronger here, though." He shifted his shoulders again and glanced briefly behind him. "It's not the most comfortable feeling."

"After my father died," Hope told him, "it seemed the one thing I really needed was to talk about him, about my memories of him. That isn't easy to do, because it makes people uncomfortable." She hesitated, then added softly, "If you'd like to talk about your memories, I'd like to hear them."

Sean said nothing for a few minutes but sat watching the flames, his face in profile to Hope.

"I always liked to have a fire in here," he said quietly. "Even in the summer, when it was hot as hell with a Santa Ana blowing. I'd beg and beg until I wore him down, and we'd sit in here, with all the windows open, sweating, while we roasted marshmallows in the fireplace." He smiled. "Whitey liked those marshmallows as much as I did. He only put up that token parental protest because he thought he was supposed to. He drank coffee in the morning, but at night he drank cocoa, out of his cocoa mug." Sean looked around. "You probably saw it—that red mug on the shelf by the sink, with his name on it in blue."

"I saw it," she murmured.

"He never used it for anything but cocoa." Sean gazed into the flames, his voice quiet, his eyes faraway as he reminisced about childhood with his flamboyant father. He was bringing Whitey to life for Hope, but he was also showing her more of himself. She thought she'd known Sean, but hearing about his childhood gave her new insight into the insecure boy who'd become the aggressively independent, self-isolating man she knew.

And as he reminisced, she felt a new closeness growing between them. She was seeing the real Sean, not the world-weary cynic he showed the world but the child inside the man, behind the facade.

He was letting her in, allowing her past the walls with which he protected himself. The things he was sharing with her, the little things, were perhaps most important of all, and Hope was both humbled and enthralled.

It was very late when Sean straightened and stretched and caught sight of the clock on the mantel.

"Good God!"

Startled, Hope pushed herself up from the sofa. "What's wrong?"

"Do you know what time it is?"

She squinted up at the mantel. "It's 12:27."

"Yeah. How did it get so late?"

"Well," she began, a teasing light in her eyes, "the big hand went around fast and the little hand went around slow and—"

"Ho, ho, ho." He shoved himself to his feet and reached down to take her hand and haul her up beside him. "Very funny. The comedians of the world can rest easy tonight, can't they?"

"I thought it was quite clever," Hope said with all the hauteur she could muster. She rose and collected their coffee cups to take them to the kitchen. "It is late, though, isn't it? I wasn't paying any attention to the time. I was too interested in listening to you."

"Don't try to con me, Hope. I've never been a riveting storyteller and I know it. That was Whitey's province."

"He may have been more flamboyant," Hope said quietly, "but I wasn't trying to con you, Sean. You painted a picture for me, helped me to see your father as he was."

"Well—" Sean seemed oddly abashed, uncomfortable with the compliment "—I'm glad I didn't bore you to death, anyway." He followed her into the kitchen.

"Just put those in the sink. We can wash them tomorrow."

"But it'll only take a—"

"No. It's late, I'm tired, and I know you're tired." Sean took her shoulders and turned her toward the doorway. "Go on upstairs. I'll lock up down here."

Hope went, looking back from three steps up the stairs to see Sean standing in the kitchen, looking at the mug he held in his hands. It was Whitey's cocoa mug.

She'd chosen the smallest of the three bedrooms, because it was tucked under the eaves at the corner of the house, papered in small pink roses, full of corners and angles, with one small dormer window facing east and one facing south. It reminded her of the kind of room she'd imagined the heroines in her storybooks having when she was small.

It was cozy upstairs, the old furnace blowing warm, slightly dusty-smelling air that admirably banished the chill and damp. Hope took her washing things to the bathroom and admired the black-and-white tile floor and the nearly antique fixtures while she washed her face and brushed her teeth. When she'd finished, she gathered her things, twitched a towel straight on the rod and opened the door right into Sean's face.

"Oh!"

She stood there, clutching her cosmetic bag and hairbrush to her breast, staring at Sean, unable to say anything more sensible than "Oh," and flushed to the roots of her hair.

Sean lowered the hand he'd raised to knock. "I'm sorry. I didn't mean to scare you."

"You—you didn't," Hope stammered. "I mean, I was—I was startled, but it wasn't your fault."

"I'm sorry I startled you, anyway." He smiled down at her. "Are you all finished?"

Hope was wearing an ankle-length cotton nightgown, sleeveless with a scoop neck but modest, under a velour robe, wrapped and belted to close high at her throat, but despite all that, she felt nearly naked under Sean's eyes. All at once it struck her that she was all alone in this house with this man, sharing a bathroom, going to bed. When they'd made their plans to come to Santa Barbara, she'd thought only of the search, not of spending the weekend alone with Sean.

It suddenly seemed very intimate, unsettlingly so.

"Y-yes. I'm finished." She glanced down at her bag and brush. "I think I have everything out of your way."

"Don't worry about it." He stepped back to allow her to pass, and she edged cautiously around him. "Just get some sleep, because we've got a long day of searching ahead of us tomorrow."

"All right." Hope paused outside her door. "Good night, Sean. And thank you for doing this for me."

He shook his head. "Don't thank me. I'm doing it as much for myself as anything."

"Thank you, anyway." She slipped through the door and closed it behind her.

The little room with its rose-covered walls and its angles and corners seemed to welcome her, and the white iron bed covered with a thick quilt looked irresistibly inviting. She laid her robe on the end of the bed, turned down the covers and switched off the lamp, but before she got into bed, she went over to the south-facing window and pulled the curtains aside to look out.

The storm still raged over the town and the ocean beyond, hurling wind and rain across the landscape, dramatic, elemental, illuminated by intermittent slashes of lightning. There was something fascinating about a storm when you were warm and dry and safe inside, and Hope didn't know how long she might have stood watching if the door hadn't opened behind her.

Sean had apparently come from the bathroom. His hair was damp, and he wore his shirt unbuttoned and loose over his slacks, as if he'd taken it off to wash and just pulled it on again to walk to his room. He didn't turn on the light, and he spoke softly, as if he thought she might be asleep.

"Hope, I—" He paused, apparently seeing that the bed was empty. "Hope?"

"I'm over here."

He whirled around when she spoke. "What?" Even in the dim light she could see him frown. "What are you doing over there?"

"Watching the storm. I didn't realize you could see all the way to the ocean from here."

"It's hard to tell from the street, but most of Santa Barbara is sloping up from the coast to the mountains. We're a fair way up the hillside here."

"It must be a spectacular view in daylight."

"It is. Once the fog burns off." Sean walked across the room to join her. He reached over her shoulder and lifted the curtain farther aside. "On a clear day, you can see a couple of the Channel Islands, Santa Cruz and Santa Rosa, from here."

"Really?" Hope looked out again, but there was nothing to be seen except the storm. "I'd love to see that. It must be beautiful."

"It is."

Sean rested a hand on her shoulder and looked past her, out at the wind and rain. His touch was light, but

Hope could feel his warmth as he stood behind her. It seemed to reach out and surround her.

"It's beautiful." His hand on her shoulder shifted, turning her with the lightest of pressure to face him. He slid his hand from her shoulder to her back, down the line of her spine to rest at her waist. "Very beautiful," he repeated, but this time he wasn't talking about the view.

He drew her closer, brushing her hair off her face with his fingertips, then sliding his hand over her head and down to cup the nape of her neck, drawing her face up to his. Hope was on her toes, off balance, and she reached forward automatically to brace her hands on Sean's chest.

His bare chest. Her hands met warm skin over hard muscle, dusted with dark hair, and she froze. Then Sean eased her a fraction closer, and her hands slipped up, over his chest, and he bent his head and found her lips with his.

Hope let him kiss her at first, following his lead, letting him show her, teach her. And then she tried, hesitantly, to show what she had learned. She parted her lips shyly and sought to answer his kisses with her own. She gripped his shoulders, and then, when he shifted his feet and pulled her still closer, she let her hands slide up and twined her arms around his neck, let her body go soft and lax, molded against the harder contours of Sean's.

He slid his hand over her back in slow circles, sliding the soft cotton of her gown against her skin. It was soothing at first, then frustrating as she began to long for the touch of his hand on her skin. He seemed to know what she wanted, what she needed, for he slid his hand up to her shoulder and along the lace that edged the neck of her gown. He traced the scooped neckline from one shoulder to the other, then slid his fingertips beneath one wide strap and eased it off her shoulder.

The strap fell onto her upper arm, and the gown slid down a fraction, clinging to the top of her breast. Sean traced the lace edging again, from her arm, across the soft upper curve of her breast, to the shadowy cleft between her breasts. He let his fingertips drift beneath the cotton to caress the velvety skin there, then slipped his hand inside to cup her breast. He brushed his thumb across the taut, tight nipple, and Hope shuddered with the sensation, her head falling back as she arched instinctively. She clung to his shoulders for support as he caressed her breasts, and when he slid both arms around her again, she returned his kisses with all her inexperienced ardor.

He didn't leave her abruptly, but when she'd have gone on to the next unknown step, he drew back, easing her gently away from passion, bringing her slowly down to earth.

"Sean?" she whispered.

"Shh." He kissed her, tenderly, not passionately. "It's late." He lifted the strap of her gown back onto her shoulder. "You need to sleep."

He steered her gently to the bed and sat her on the side, then left her. At the door he paused. "Good night, Hope. Sleep well." And he was gone.

Hope looked over at the window and saw that the storm had passed. The rain had gone, the wind was falling and the moon was swimming out from behind the last ragged clouds, washing the sky with silver.

"Rise and shine, sleepyhead!" The obnoxiously cheerful call resounded through the bedroom.

Hope buried her face in the pillow and tried to ignore the racket. "Don't want to," she muttered into the pillow.

The door shook under a volley of knocks. "Come on, get up! We've got a house to search!"

The search! Hope's head snapped up and she tumbled out of bed, blinking against the brilliant sunlight that streamed in the east window, wide awake in the moment it took for the thought to penetrate.

"I'm awake!" she called through the door. "I'm up! Don't start looking without me, okay?"

"Okay!" She could hear the smile in Sean's voice as he replied. "I brought a cup of coffee up. I'll put it on this little table out here, all right?"

"All right. And thank you!"

"Don't thank me, just hurry!"

Hope listened to his retreating footsteps for a moment, then she hurried, arriving downstairs showered, dressed, combed and brushed in just under twelve minutes. It took another fifteen for them to share the scrambled eggs and toast Sean had fixed and wash their few dishes.

When the kitchen was neat again, Sean led the way into the living room, stood in the middle of it with hands on hips and looked around.

"Well?" he asked. "Where should we start?"

Hope considered for a moment. "You knew him," she said. "Was he a *Purloined Letter* type or a *Treasure Island* type?"

"Do you mean would he hide something in plain sight or bury it away somewhere?"

Hope nodded.

Sean considered that for a moment, then shrugged. "To be honest, I don't know."

"Oh." Hope looked around at all the shelves and cupboards in that room alone and considered the possibility of attics and basements, as well. Her shoulders sagged a little, but then she straightened them and lifted her chin. "I guess we might as well be systematic about it, then. Do you want to start on the left side of the fireplace or the right?"

"If we're going to be systematic, we might as well go around the room clockwise. Let's start on the right." He strode to the right side of the fireplace and began lifting books down from the top shelf.

Hope took the books he handed her, looked to see that each was what it appeared to be and no more, and, when a whole shelf had been checked, handed them back to be replaced.

The work required little thought and no concentration and quickly developed an automatic rhythm. There was time for thought of other things, for conversation, for observation.

And they were observing each other.

Something profound had changed between them last night, and though neither spoke about it, they were both aware.

They were different. Where they had been a little stiff with each other before, a little reserved, a little suspicious, they were more relaxed now, comfortable rather than guarded.

A new sort of tension was growing between them now, the tension that exists between two people who are seeing each other as a man and a woman.

Hope could see it in Sean's actions, in the way he touched her shoulder lightly to get her attention or brushed a lock of hair off her forehead. She could see it in the way he refused to let her lift anything heavy, in the way he reached around her to assist when she held something awkward, in the way he steadied her with a hand at her waist when she took her turn standing on the footstool to reach the higher shelves.

His eyes were warm when he looked at her, and even his voice seemed a fraction lower, the timbre slightly more husky when he spoke. Something about him this morning emboldened Hope so that she dared to touch Sean in return, to straighten his collar and rub a smudge of dust off his cheek, to reach for his hand when she mounted the stool instead of simply clambering up.

She felt a new excitement, a sense of heightened anticipation growing in her, that had nothing to do with Whitey's papers.

Sean didn't want to take his eyes off her. He had to force himself to face the bookshelves, to take down the dusty volumes one by one and replace them when they'd been checked. He didn't want to handle books, insisted his wayward thoughts, he wanted to handle Hope. He wanted to throw the damned books aside and carry her upstairs to the little east-facing bedroom and make love to her in the sunlight that poured through the windows in the wake of last night's storm.

There had been a storm inside last night as well as out, and he knew that something fundamental had changed between them. He only hoped he could cope with the change, when the last thing on earth he wanted to do was cope.

She'd probably be shocked to death if she knew what he was thinking, but just being near her was driving him crazy. Every time she looked at him with eyes the clear, pure green of emeralds, alight with what he thought was the excitement of the search, he wanted to kiss her. Her cheeks were softly flushed with her exertions, her lips soft and pink. Even her movements seemed different, more supple, fluid, with a little sway to her hips, a flirtatious tilt to her head.

He wondered if she knew she was driving him crazy. He couldn't resist touching her, though he tried to keep the touches impersonal, turning her with a hand on her shoulder or brushing her hair out of her eyes. Each touch aroused a memory, though, of other touches, of silken skin and soft hair and the fascinating, tantalizing juxtaposition of naiveté and passion.

She was beautiful. She was fascinating. She was naive and intelligent and passionate and sweet.

And she was off-limits.

Chapter 11

Dinner was late, for they were both reluctant to interrupt the search. It was hunger and fatigue that finally forced them to take a break. They had Sean's favorite, carryout Chinese from a restaurant at the foot of the hill, and sat in front of the fireplace to eat it.

After searching all the rooms on the main floor of the house, they'd climbed the attic stairs at seven-thirty that evening, looked at the chaos beneath the rafters and made the mutual decision that the attic could wait. They'd taken turns showering off the dust and sweat of the search, and then while Sean drove down the hill for the food, Hope got out dishes and cutlery and made a pot of tea.

"Mmm." Sitting on the braided rug in front of the sofa, Hope ate her last bite of chicken and broccoli and leaned back against the sofa, cradling her cup of tea in her hands. "That was good."

"Yeah." Sean leaned back beside her, his shoulder brushing hers, his legs stretched out alongside hers. "We didn't just need that food, we needed a break."

"Mmm." Hope sipped her tea. "I can't believe that attic."

"It shouldn't have come as a surprise after seeing his office in L.A."

"Probably not, but I really didn't know you could fit that much stuff in an attic. And how did he get that moose head up those narrow little stairs, anyway?"

"Beats me." Sean grinned. "I was wondering how that monster sofa got up there. There's no way it would have fit up the stairway."

"I can't imagine. That's quite a collection we have to search through up there."

"Because..." Sean began, and Hope finished the thought in laughing chorus with him, the phrase that had become their touchstone as they plowed through the accumulated relics of Whitey Baker's life.

"...he never threw anything away!"

Sean draped an arm around her shoulders, and Hope let herself snuggle closer, still chuckling.

"It would have been a shame, you know, if you'd sold this house and never seen all the stuff that's in it."

"A shame or a relief?" Sean wondered.

"A shame." She rested her head on his shoulder. "This is your father's life. Through these things he left, you have a chance to know him."

"For the pack rat that he was, right?"

"I'm serious, Sean."

"I know you are." He sighed. "And I am, too, really. There's so much I never knew about my father. We let so much time go past, we let all the chances go past, until there were no more chances left. You don't think about the fact, while that time, those chances, are passing, that you will never have them again. You get so busy living your life day to day, wrapped up in trivialities, putting the important things off until later. You get so busy that you forget that once it's gone, you can never get that time back. And then all at once it's too late to do the things, say the things, that you wanted to and never did. And all you're left with is regrets."

"And memories," Hope offered. "You have the memories, and nothing can ever take that away."

"Yeah." He watched the fire for a time. "But you were there with your father, all the time."

"And you think that means I don't have regrets? There was nothing I left unsaid?" Hope shook her head. "Everyone has regrets, Sean. Perhaps some more than others, but I think everyone is left with the feeling that if they'd had just a little more time, just one more chance, they could have said it all or done it all. I felt that way, but I don't think it's true. For those who are left behind the time is always too short."

"So you're telling me that there's always one more thing you would have said or done, and not to beat myself up about it?" he asked, lifting his head and looking down at her face.

"I'm telling you that when you lose someone, it's always too soon. You want more time with them, another chance."

"That's what I want. I want all those years back, all the time we wasted over something that seems so trivial now."

"You mustn't be so hard on yourself, Sean. You had those last weeks with him. That's more than many people get."

"Yes, but—"

"No buts." Hope reached up and laid a finger across his lips. "Don't waste time on regrets, Sean. Be glad for what you had, because you had more than many people do."

He took her hand and pressed a kiss into her palm. "I did, didn't I?"

"Mmm-hmm." She nodded.

"And I am grateful for that, you know." He kissed the thin skin of her inner wrist.

"I know you are."

"You do, huh?" He smiled gently, the firelight casting flickering shadows over his features, seeming to light his dark eyes from within. "You seem to know a lot."

Hope just smiled and lowered her eyes.

"How did you get so wise, anyway?" Sean stroked her shoulder, then trailed his fingertips up the side of her neck and into her hair. "Where did you learn so much about life?"

"By living it." Hope leaned into his caress. "How else does anyone learn about life?"

"But you're so young."

"No, I'm not," she corrected him. "You seem to see me as a child, Sean, but I'm not."

"Not?" he murmured.

"Not." She shook her head, her hair swinging onto his shoulder. "I'm not a child. I'm a woman. I wish it wasn't so hard for you to look at me and see that."

His fingers in her hair moved, tipping her face up to his. She looked up from beneath the screen of her lashes and found him watching her with a small smile tugging at the corner of his mouth.

"It's not all that hard to see," he murmured. "As a matter of fact, it's getting easier all the time." He bent his head only a fraction, all that was needed to cover her lips with his.

She was pliant and warm in his arms, and he drew her around and down to lie with him on the braided rug before the fire. He propped himself on one elbow, looking down at her in the firelight. He drew his fingers softly through her hair, smoothing it back from her face.

"I do know that you're not a child," he whispered, and kissed her, long and slow and deep. He lifted his head. "But I wonder if you really want this."

"Don't wonder." Hope reached up to pull him down for another kiss, longer this time, and deeper, and if possible, even sweeter. When the kiss ended, she drew back a fraction, smoothing Sean's hair back off his forehead. "I know what I want." She slid the pad of her thumb across his lips. "And you know what I want."

"I know what you think you want." He studied her face from that very close angle for a moment, then heaved himself away, rolling over onto his back beside her. "But I don't think you know what's good for you."

"What?" Hope thought he might reach for her, but he folded his arms across his chest. "What are you talking about?"

"You. Me. Us." He waved his hand, encompassing them and the room around them. "This. What we both want. What I think would hurt you."

Hope rolled onto her elbow, watching his face. "Why don't you let me worry about what will hurt me, Sean?"

"Because I want to take care of you."

"Don't." She reached out, and though he'd crossed his arms, physically closing himself off from her, she took his hand and clasped it in hers. "Don't do this, Sean. Don't try to wrap me up in tissue paper and hide me away from real life. You must know you can't do that, however hard you try."

He was shaking his head in denial of her words. "You're so innocent. You're not ready for this."

"I am ready. I love you, Sean."

"Don't." His reply was quick and curt. "Don't love me, Hope."

"I do. You must know that."

"I hoped you wouldn't. You don't want to love me, because I don't have anything to give you but hurt."

"You have so much to give. You've given me so much already, how can you say that?"

"Because I know. I'll hurt you without meaning to, without wanting to. My kind of life is no good for you. I'm no good for you."

"You are so wrong." She tightened her grip on his hand and waited until he turned to look at her. "I'm not afraid of hurt, Sean. Hurt is a part of life."

"God, Hope, you're so young! What do you know about life?"

"I know about life. I watched my father die."

"I know," he said after a moment. "I'm sorry."

"Don't be. Death is a part of life. Grief is natural, so is hurt. You learn from them, you survive them. You deal with them, and you grow."

Sean rolled onto his side so they were face-to-face. "You think you're so grown-up," he murmured, "but you've never done this before, have you?"

She flushed and fought the urge to hide her face. "No," she finally whispered, "I haven't. Does that make a difference to you?"

He frowned. "To me? It's you it should make a difference to. This is a big decision, Hope."

"It's my decision," she said quietly. "You can't make it for me, Sean. Unless you...you don't want me...because it's the first time?"

His laugh was more like a groan. "If you don't know I want you, you're even more innocent than I thought."

"Then you don't mind...that I never..."

He shook his head, then traced a fingertip lightly down her cheek. "I don't want to hurt you. And I will."

"You don't know that. And it's not for you to worry about what I should be afraid of. I've tried to tell you that."

"But I—"

"I'm not a china doll. I won't break if you touch me." She eased closer and laid one hand on his cheek. "I'm a woman, Sean. I won't break if you touch me." She stroked his cheek, then his lips, lightly, delicately. "But I think I may die if you don't touch me."

Sean took her fingertip between his lips for a brief kiss, and then, with a soft groan of surrender, he rolled her into his arms, kissing her with all the passion he'd tried so hard to suppress.

Afterward, Hope was never sure if Sean had carried her upstairs or if she'd walked. She remembered only disconnected images, like sharp, clear photographs taken through the haze of passion. She remembered the moonlight, pouring through the octagonal window above the stair landing, silvering Sean's hair and the hard planes of his face when he lifted his lips from hers to look down at her for a moment. She remembered the little bedroom where they stood together in another pool of moonlight, pouring through the window that looked out to the sea; where she slid Sean's shirt off his shoulders, watching, with a hunger she hadn't known she was capable of, the way the moonlight gleamed on the smooth skin of his shoulders.

She remembered watching the flex and bunch of heavy muscle as he reached out to unbutton her sweater, remembered the exquisitely gentle touch of strong hands on her body, remembered that she'd felt no embarrassment or awkwardness when he stripped away the last of her clothing and looked at her body. She'd felt pride that he found her beautiful, and a hunger to match the hunger she saw in his eyes, and a newly awakening feminine power to excite.

It was both exalting and humbling to know that this strong man wanted her, that his hands trembled slightly when he touched her, that he groaned aloud when she touched him, shyly at first, then with more assurance as she learned that she pleased him.

And then she remembered the heat of skin against skin, the cool, smooth sheets against her back, Sean's hands and lips on her body and a spiraling tension and need that wound tighter and tighter within her. The tension grew until she thought she'd break apart from it, and then, at that moment when she could no longer bear the tension, came the release. She wasn't aware of tangibles, only of heat and light and waves of sensation that blotted out everything else.

And then, as she slid into sleep, she remembered the sense of safety she felt, wrapped in Sean's arms. This was the man she loved, the man who was now her lover, and in his arms she found a depth of fulfillment and security she knew she would find nowhere else.

He murmured something, close to her ear, and it wasn't until later that she realized she'd understood what he said.

"Don't love me, Hope," he whispered. "Don't love me."

She woke slowly, easing gradually out of sleep, reluctant to open her eyes and make that commitment to wakefulness. She shifted and stretched and came up against something warm and very solid.

"Good morning, Hope."

Her eyes snapped open as the words rumbled deep beneath her ear. The shadows of the night had gone, literally and figuratively. Early morning sunshine poured through the east window, and Sean's expression was free from the shadows of warning or regret. He smiled gently at her confusion.

"Sleep well?"

She lifted her head from Sean's chest and smiled shyly up at him through the screen of her lashes. "Yes," she whispered, then bent her head and hid her face again, mortified to feel herself blushing.

"Hey—" Sean's voice was warm with amusement "—you don't have to hide from me. Come here." He slipped his fingers beneath her chin and gently lifted her face. "I have to say good-morning to you," he told her, and kissed her lips.

The fire was still there, she found, smoldering, waiting only for Sean's kiss to stir the embers into flame. It licked along her veins as she turned into his arms, winding her arms around his neck, her legs tangling with his as the fire burned high, taking them down into its midst again.

It was sunlight that poured across the bed when they resurfaced, warming the room, warming them. Sean had pulled the sheet across them as they drifted together into a light sleep, but they'd twisted it around them, baring one of Hope's legs and Sean's broad chest. She woke from the brief nap and stretched luxuriously, reveling in the warmth, in the sense of sated, fulfilled relaxation that suffused her.

Her movements must have awakened Sean, for he blinked his eyes open and smiled at her. "Are you hungry?"

She blushed and ducked her head, wondering if love and wanting could really show that clearly in her face.

"I mean for breakfast!" Sean clarified with a chuckle, confirming her belief that he could see right through her. "Eggs, pancakes, stuff like that?"

"I know," she mumbled into the pillow. "And now that you mention it, I'm starving!"

"Me, too." He kissed her bare shoulder above the sheet, then slid out of bed. Hope heard a rustle as he retrieved his jeans from the floor, then the rasp of the zipper. "Do you care if I take first shower?"

She looked up from the pillow. "Of course not."

"Okay." He scooped his shirt up from the armchair where it had landed. "I'll be out in a couple of minutes, and by the time you're done up here, breakfast will be ready."

"Sean, you don't need to cook for me—" Hope began, but she was too late.

Sean's prediction was accurate. By the time she was showered, dressed and downstairs, he had plates of scrambled eggs and bacon on the table, along with juice and coffee.

He turned from a skillet full of pancakes and looked over his shoulder when she walked into the room, smiling at her before he turned back to the stove. "If you want milk for your coffee, there's plenty in the refrigerator."

"Okay. Shall I get some for you?"

"Yeah, if you would. Pour half an inch or so in my cup, okay?"

"Right." She poured the milk, smiling, enjoying the little intimacy, wondering if this was how married people felt in the morning. Wondering if they knew how special it was to share breakfast with someone they loved. How much more special would it be if he loved her in return?

For she did love Sean Boudreaux. She'd told him the simple truth last night, that she loved him, that she hungered to make love with him. And that she had no more voluntary control over that love than she had over the next earthquake.

If anything, she loved him more this morning for his kindness and his consideration of her, and for his acceptance, at long last, that she was an adult, capable of making the decision to become his lover.

When she poured milk in his coffee, she was doing it for the man she loved, and when she pulled the kitchen curtains aside to look out at a brilliant, sunny morning, she needed to share her bubbling, fizzing joy with him. A cascade of trumpet vine spilled from the eaves above down one side of the window, and a hummingbird hung there, darting from one flower to another, jewel-bright feathers glinting in the sunlight.

"Sean!" Hope whispered, standing very still. "Look!"

"What is it?" He had his back to her, scooping the last of the pancakes from the skillet.

"A hummingbird. Look!"

"Really?" He turned from the stove, plate in hand.

"Don't scare him!" she whispered, waving him over with gestures she hoped were small enough not to alarm the bird.

"Scare a hummingbird?" Sean slipped his arms around her waist from behind and bent to rest his chin on her shoulder, looking out at the tiny bird. "Do you know how ferocious those little guys are?"

"Oh, yes." Hope nodded. "We had them around the convent in Mexico. The local alley cats were terrified of them."

"They dive-bombed the cats to run them off?"

"Yes, but how did you know?"

"They do the same thing to coyotes on the hill behind my house. A ninth of an ounce of pure fury."

Together they watched as the bird sipped from one last flower, then with a deepening of the low buzz of his wings, he backed away from the vine and zoomed off. When he'd gone, Hope turned in Sean's arms to kiss him, seeing surprise in his eyes, and then the darkening smokiness that she was coming to recognize as dawning passion. When the kiss ended she let her arms slip away reluctantly, hungry once again for more than breakfast.

"Come on and eat this," Sean urged briskly, "before it gets cold." He steered her from the window back to the table, where he plopped her in a chair.

Hope unfolded her napkin across her lap, while Sean shoveled food onto a plate. She didn't think much about what he was doing until he set the plate in front of *her*.

"Sean, what *is* all this?" She stared at the mounds of food.

"Your breakfast."

"You're kidding."

"I am absolutely serious." He dived into his own breakfast with gusto. "Go on—" he waved a fork at her plate "—eat up."

She took a bite. "This is very good."

"Glad you like it."

"But, Sean, for future reference..."

"Hmm?"

"I can't eat this much in a whole day, never mind for breakfast!"

He glanced at her, then at her plate, and grinned. "You need your strength."

Hope looked at him warily. "I'm almost afraid to ask, but is there a reason why I need my strength?"

He nodded. "Yeah. There is."

Hope waited for him to add more, but he didn't. "Okay," she said at last, "I'll bite. What's the reason that I need a Paul Bunyan breakfast to keep my strength up?"

Sean smiled like a man with several aces up his sleeve. "Whitey's attic."

"Oh, boy," Hope sighed an hour later, "you weren't exaggerating, were you?"

"Given what we already know about Whitey's storage philosophy, did I need to exaggerate?"

Sean stood on a stool, examining the contents of a tall bookcase, while Hope perched on an upended orange crate and rummaged through a deep, dusty, steamer trunk. She pulled out a shoe box tied shut with string and sneezed as a cloud of dust drifted up.

"No." She shook her head, then sneezed again and rubbed her nose, leaving a streak of dust. "After all we've seen, there's no reason for either of us to be sur-

prised at this.'' She began working at the knots holding
the shoe box closed. ''Have you found anything?''

''About the same as you. Four zillion old books, a
box full of incomplete decks of playing cards and another box full of old doorknobs.''

''Old doorknobs?'' The first of the knots came loose,
and Hope started on the second. ''Why would he keep
old doorknobs?''

''Why did he keep any of this?'' Shaking his head,
Sean set a stack of books aside and started on the next
shelf. ''The man wanted to be known as eccentric. He
took the concept to new heights. He must have thought
one of the hallmarks of eccentricity was—''

''Sean!''

''—hoarding worthless junk.''

''Sean, look!''

''I have to admit I can't—''

''Sean, *look at this!*'' Hope almost shouted. ''Forget about the doorknobs and *look at this!*''

She held up the shoe box, open at last. ''Look!''

He looked and saw that the box was filled to the brim
with photographs.

''Pictures?''

''Yes, but look at what they're pictures of! Just
look!'' She got up and hurried across to him with the
box. ''Look at these!''

The pictures were old, black-and-white snapshots
from the forties with funny, wavy-cut edges.

''Looks who's in them!'' Hope insisted, holding one
up for Sean to see.

''My father?'' he said slowly, taking the print from
her.

''Yes, but look who else!'' She pointed to the other
man in the photo, a tall, lean man with thinning hair,

standing with his arm around Whitey's shoulders, smiling for the camera.

Sean shook his head. "I don't know who the other guy is. I don't think I've ever seen him."

"I have." Hope smiled and touched the man's image delicately with her fingertip, almost a caress. "It's *my* father."

Chapter 12

"Your father?"

"My father," she replied.

Sean lifted her hand, turning it so the light caught the picture as he looked closer. "Your father and mine," he murmured.

"Together," Hope added.

"When was this taken?"

Sean slipped the picture from her fingers and turned it over. "October '47" was written in the corner in a small, neat hand.

"Do you know whose handwriting that is?" he asked.

Hope shook her head. "I've never seen it."

"It's my mother's." Shaking his head in wonder, he turned the picture over and studied the image again. "I can't believe it."

"There's more, though." Hope lifted the box to show him. "All the pictures I've seen in here so far are of our parents. If this is your mother, that is."

She showed him another print, of the two men and a pretty, smiling woman dressed in a full-skirted shirt-waist dress in the style of the late forties.

"That's her."

"She's very pretty."

"Yeah." Sean smiled. "She still is, even now. It must come of spending all her time playing golf in Florida."

"I don't remember my mother. I've only seen pictures of her," Hope said.

Sean looked among the pictures still in the box for a moment and extracted one. "Is this her?"

"Yes." Hope took it from him, studying the young woman sitting with Whitey and Philip at a picnic table. "Yes, that's her."

"You look like her."

"Do I?" She looked quickly up at Sean, her eyes wide and soft. "Do I really?"

"You do. Around the mouth—" he traced her features lightly with a fingertip "—and the chin and the eyebrows. Were her eyes green?"

"My father said they were. He said when he looked at my eyes he could almost see her looking out of them." Her smile was a bit sad. "I thought it was a compliment when I was little, but it must have caused him pain to look at me and know she was dead."

"Or it caused him joy to know that, even after her death, a part of her lived on."

Sean shuffled through the pictures, laying them out on a dust-sheet-covered shape they'd discovered was an end table with a particularly ugly mother-of-pearl inlaid top. He sorted through the pictures by their subject, separating those in which both Whitey and Philip appeared.

They made a significant stack, perhaps three dozen photos in all, with the dates written neatly on the backs, from 1946 to 1951.

Sean looked up from the pictures. "What year was your father subpoenaed?"

"1951."

"And he went to Mexico that year?"

"In August of 1951, yes."

"The latest picture in this bunch is dated July 4, 1951. This one," he said quietly, lifting one of Philip and Whitey standing by a low stone wall. "That was taken here. In the backyard."

"Was it?" Hope looked more closely at the picture, then stepped over to the small attic window to look down at the backyard. "It doesn't look the same."

"Picture all those big trees as little bitty twigs," Sean suggested. "They were standing over there, by the corner of the wall."

After a moment, Hope nodded. "Yes, I see. Forty years makes a difference, doesn't it?"

"Usually does."

"It's so wonderful to see these and know that he and my mother were actually here."

"He was actually here," Sean repeated, almost to himself. "He and Whitey were obviously friends. All these pictures." He shook his head. "My God, it's actually true."

"Of course it's true." Hope tenderly gathered up some pictures of her parents. "I told you it was true."

"So you did." Sean looked at her with a newly assessing light in his eyes. "You told me and told me, but it just seemed too farfetched to believe."

He reached out for her hand and drew her toward him, sliding his arm around her shoulders and pulling her close to kiss her tenderly.

"Do you think you can forgive me?" he asked when he lifted his head. "I didn't believe you."

"There's nothing to forgive." Hope reached up and kissed him again, a brief, light touch. "In your position, I probably wouldn't have believed it, either. Looking at it objectively, it really doesn't make sense, does it?"

"Not really," Sean agreed, "but who ever said life made sense?"

Hope shrugged.

"Nobody." He looked from the pictures to their cluttered surroundings. "And now that we've found this much, we'd better get busy on the rest. There's still a lot to search."

That was an understatement of heroic proportions, and not even the encouraging impetus of the pictures could alter the fact that there was too much to search and too little time.

They worked feverishly to do all they could before eight o'clock, which was when Sean had said they must leave, but at five-thirty, hunger forced them to take a break for a quick supper of pizza and soda.

They'd finished with the attic and had reached the basement by that time, and the last thing Hope found before the pizza delivery man rang the doorbell was a big carton of paperback mysteries. She carried them upstairs to look through the box while they ate, chuckling at the lurid covers and hokey titles.

"These are hilarious, Sean! Look at this one—*Cave of the Werewolf*! Did Whitey really read this stuff?"

"You bet he did." Sean took the book and turned it over to read the blurb on the back cover. "He loved 'em. He used to read them to me, acting out all the scary parts. He especially liked stuff about hidden passages and secret compartments and things, and—" Sean broke off abruptly.

"And what?" Hope asked absently. She finished off her piece of pizza and took another mystery out of the box, shaking her head over the picture on the cover of a scantily dressed young woman fleeing a large, featureless monster.

"That's it," he murmured to himself.

"What did you say?" Hope was reading what the back cover had to say about the lady and the monster.

"That's it!" Sean grabbed the book from her hands and pulled her out of her chair to spin her across the kitchen in an exuberant dance. "Hope, *that's it!*" He kissed her hard, swinging her around so that her feet left the floor.

"What's what?" she gasped, clutching his shoulders for dear life as he whirled her around the room. "Sean, what are you talking about?" On their third circuit of the kitchen, Hope managed to plant her feet and bring them to a halt, though Sean still swayed irrepressibly to the beat of some unseen orchestra.

"Whitey and his mysteries!" He kissed her again, and Hope clung to him, letting the passion sweep through her for that moment. He was laughing when he lifted his lips. "We've been going at it all wrong, Hope. If he had anything to hide, he wouldn't have left it in a file or a box somewhere, he'd have hidden it, like in his mysteries! He'd have hidden it in a secret compartment or a hidden passage or something like that!"

"A secret compartment?" she repeated dubiously.

"Of course! Whitey was crazy about stories of secret hiding places. It would be just like him to have a secret compartment of his own in the wall or a hidden door in the paneling or something. All we have to do is find it!"

Just find it. That was all. The problem with finding a hidden compartment, Hope pointed out an hour later, was that a hidden compartment was designed to stay hidden. They'd spent that hour feverishly tugging on door frames and pressing bookcase shelves, to no avail, and were running out of both patience and places to look.

"Did he have a particular favorite as far as types of secret compartments go?" she wondered a little desperately. "I mean, did he prefer secret doors in the paneling or trapdoors under rugs or something?"

Sean shook his head. "He liked them all. I can't remember any special favorite." He abandoned the bookshelf above the window and stepped down from the stool he'd been standing on. "Nothing up there but books and dust."

"Nothing down here, either." Hope gave up on an ornately carved cabinet that had looked like just the thing to be covered with secret switches. It wasn't. "All this carving is just that...carving."

"At least we've ruled it out." Sean dusted his hands together, sending a cloud swirling into the air. He sneezed. "Now where in this room have we *not* looked?"

They looked and said it together, "The fireplace."

The massive stone construction nearly filled the wall with a raised stone hearth in front of the firebox, a broad chimneypiece rising to the ceiling and a thick stone mantel running from one side to the other. It was built to dominate the room, fashioned of jagged, irregular stone, with room only for a narrow bookcase on either side.

"Then we start with the fireplace." Sean moved to the left side, motioning Hope to the right.

"What do we look for?" Hope experimentally pushed on a slab of gray stone with a rose-colored streak running through it. It felt as solid as the mountains outside.

"Loose stones, I guess. Or things that wiggle or turn when you push on them. Or pull on them." Sean was pushing and pulling and wiggling as he spoke. "Anything that isn't a solid stone fireplace, I suppose."

"Any of these stones?" Hope looked up at the seemingly solid wall rising to the ceiling.

"Come on." Sean crossed to her and took her in his arms. "You can't give up on me now, not after all we've already done."

"I can't?" Hope asked, weary and a bit forlorn.

"You can't." Sean kissed her, once quickly, then a second time, long and sweet. "You're too brave and too determined to give up now." He lifted his head and looked down at her. "Aren't you?"

After a moment, Hope smiled. "I guess I am."

"Then let's get to it."

It was tedious work, pressing and pulling and wiggling and twisting each of hundreds of stones, but they kept at it systematically. When Hope's determination flagged, Sean was there to keep her going, and when Sean grew discouraged, Hope was there to cheer him on.

She'd worked her way across her half of the raised hearth and was halfway up the side of the chimney-piece, when a slab of stone wobbled in her hands. Her searching had become so much by rote, push-pull-twist-wiggle, that for a moment she didn't realize what had happened. She moved on to the next stone, then froze as realization struck.

That rock, that last rock, had moved when she pulled on it.

She snatched her hands away from the masonry and stared at the one that had moved. It looked just like all the rest, didn't it? Except...was it perhaps sticking out just a little bit farther than the others? It was hard to be sure, since the wall had been deliberately constructed in a ragged, irregular style.

Slowly, almost fearfully, she gripped the stone again. She wiggled it...pulled on it and felt it move toward her. It moved only a fraction before it grated and stuck, but it definitely moved.

"Sean."

It came out as barely a whisper, and he didn't hear.

"Sean!"

"What?" He grunted as he tugged on a particularly large slab of stone, set immovably among the rest.

"Come here." Hope still spoke barely above a whisper. "Look at this rock!" She didn't look up, almost afraid to take her eyes off the rock lest it disappear or refuse to move again.

"Look at what?" Sean gave his stone a last, exasperated shove.

"Look at this stone, Sean. This big one, right here. It moved!"

"What?" His voice sharpened as what she'd said actually penetrated.

"This stone moves!" She tugged again, and it grated out another fraction of an inch. "Look at it! It moves!"

"Good God, it does!" He was at her side in two long strides. "Do that again, pull on it."

Hope took her hands away and folded them together. "No. You do it."

He shook his head. "You found it. You should be the one to pull it out."

"I don't know if it'll come all the way out."

"There's only one way to find out." He put an arm around her shoulders and urged her back up to face the stone. "Pull on it."

"Okay..." Hope grasped the rock with both hands, braced herself and pulled, wiggling the rock when it stuck on its neighbors.

Sean stayed behind her, his hands on her waist, and reached around her to take the weight of the stone as they eased it free of the wall of rock. It was jagged and rough in front, and apparently one of the biggest stones in the wall, but it was oddly light for its apparent size.

The reason for that became clear when Sean took it from Hope's hands and set it on the floor. The back of the rock had been cut away, carefully hollowed out to leave a good-sized space where no apparent space existed.

Hope stared at the carved-out rock, then at Sean, whose stunned expression mirrored her own, and finally at the black gap in the stone wall.

Sean whistled under his breath, long and low. He ran his fingers around the outside of the stone, then around the inside of the gap in the wall.

"Nice work." He took Hope's hand and ran her fingers over the mortar at the edge of the opening. "Feel how smooth that is?"

"Mmm-hmm."

"That's not easy to do. Somebody knew what they were doing when they built this."

"Whitey?"

Sean shrugged. "Maybe. He wasn't big on home repairs, but he could do the handyman-type things when he had a good reason to. It's my guess he'd consider a secret compartment a hell of a reason."

"But what's in there?" Hope bent to peer inside but could see only darkness. "It could be nothing more than a loose stone, couldn't it?"

"Not with the back of the stone carved out like it is," he disagreed. "This was done for a reason."

"Is there anything in there?" She bent to peer at the dark gap, too, but she didn't reach out to put her hand in it.

"Don't know yet." Sean rested his hand on the edge, then paused and grinned up at her. "You know, there's something really creepy about putting your hand in a dark hole. What if there's something in there, something with sharp teeth?"

"Like a mouse?"

"Yeah. Or a squirrel. Or a bat."

"Not a bat!" She shuddered and stepped quickly back.

"What's the matter? Is Hope scared of an innocent little bat?" He chuckled. "They're just—"

"I know. They're nothing but flying mice and they eat insects and we should all be grateful to them. I know all that, but there's something instinctive that tells me that bats are icky." She looked at him with pleading eyes. "Tell me there's not a bat in there, okay?"

"I can't really tell you what there is in there." He bent and peered inside. "It seems to go a long way back." Hope held her breath when he put his hand inside, but it appeared there was nothing with sharp teeth waiting in there after all. Sean put his arm in to the elbow, and after a few moments of searching around, he sat back on his heels.

"Huh."

"What is it? What's in there?"

"There's a dial of some kind, like on a combination lock." He looked up at her. "I can turn it, but how are you supposed to open a combination lock if you can't see the numbers on the dial?"

"With a stethoscope, like safecrackers in movies do?"

He slid her a very wry look. "Yeah, right. So what do I do? Just toddle down to Santa Barbara Memorial Hospital and tell them I need a stethoscope to open a safe? I'd be lucky if I didn't end up in jail!"

"There must be some way to open it, then."

Hope squeezed in beside him and reached into the dark opening. Because she was squashed in beside Sean and reaching in from an angle, it was she who felt the other stone move.

"Sean! This one's loose, too!"

He'd heard the grating and was already drawing it out as she pulled her arm out of the way. It was another large stone, not hollowed at the back this time, but flat, artificially smoothed. With it out, they could both see the door of a gray metal safe, with the combination dial in the middle of it.

There was a little rust around the edges of the door, but when Hope reached in and twisted the dial, it turned easily. She pulled her arm out and sat back on her heels.

"I can't believe it."

"Just like one of his mysteries," Sean agreed.

"There's only one problem." Hope looked up at Sean. "What's the combination?"

"It has to be something easy," Sean said briskly. "Whitey had a rotten memory for numbers."

"How easy? One right, two left, three right?"

"Not necessarily that easy, but maybe a birthday or something. Might as well try." He began dialing with Whitey's birthday and struck gold on his third try. The combination turned out to be Sean's own birthday, a discovery that left him oddly touched.

"I wouldn't have thought he'd even remember it," he told Hope, his voice just a little bit husky. He cleared his throat. "I always got birthday presents, but they were always sent by his secretary. I figured she had my birthday written down and sent something automatically. I never thought he actually knew it."

"He must have known he'd remember it or he wouldn't have used it as the combination."

"I keep finding out how little I knew him," Sean said quietly. "I wonder what else I didn't know." He grasped the safe handle and pulled, and with a piercing squeak it opened.

"Well I'll be damned."

The safe was good-sized and stuffed full of papers. Sean pulled them out, slowly at first, then a handful at a time, until the safe was empty and there was enough to fill a file box stacked on the floor in front of them. There were envelopes full of memos and folders filled with correspondence, sheaves of notes in Whitey's nearly indecipherable scrawl and stacks of scripts held together with string or with rubber bands that had crumbled with age.

Hope opened a folder and read for a moment, then laughed aloud. "Did you know your father wanted to have a cartoon character like Mickey Mouse? Listen to this. 'Tell J if Disney can do it, so can we! I want a mouse!!!!' And he puts four exclamation points after that!''

"I know. With all the movies he made, it always bugged him that he never came up with an animated character that caught the public's fancy." Sean glanced at the memo, then set it aside. "I wonder why he thought that had to be stored in a safe?"

"I wonder what else he thought should be kept in a safe?"

They lifted items from the pile, one by one, slowly, a little awed by their discovery.

It was Hope who found the ledger, tucked inside an expandable file full of loose sheets of paper and secured with a shoestring. She opened it with no unusual interest and gasped when she read the first entries.

"Sean, look! Here it is! It's Whitey's record of payments to Philip!" She held out the book. "See? He didn't even put these in code!"

"Centurion." Sean read the heading at the top of the page, then the first entry on a page filled with similar notations: "$1,500 to Phil C., August 12, '52."

Other pages were headed with the names of movies Hope had insisted her father wrote, and Sean read the list with growing amazement, stunned, barely able to take it in. If Sean was stunned, though, Hope was radiant, glowing with the vindication of her long-held dream. When he handed her the ledger, she hugged it against her breast.

"This is it," she whispered. "This is the proof."

Sean shook his head as he lifted a few folders and let them slide back onto the pile. "So it's really true," he murmured. "Unbelievable."

"What else is there?" Hope demanded. Still clutching the ledger, she rummaged one-handed among the papers.

"Who knows?" Sean caught her hand before she could thoroughly scramble the stack. "But we don't have time to go through all of it now."

"We don't? Oh, come on, Sean. We can't stop now. We have to see what's here!"

"We will see, but not here, not now."

"Why not?" she protested, leaning forward to lay her arms protectively across the papers.

"Because if we don't head back to L.A. within the next half hour, you aren't going to get to work in the morning."

"Oh." Hope looked at her watch. "Oh!" She scrambled to her feet. "Good grief, it's almost midnight! When did it get so late?"

"Probably while we were trying out our skills as safe breakers," Sean replied. "How fast can you pack?"

"Is five minutes fast enough?"

"Should be." He rose and pulled her to her feet beside him. "We can put all this in one of those boxes from the attic. We'll take it back to L.A. and then go through it all tomorrow."

Hope looked at it longingly. "I wish we could go through it now."

"We know that Whitey's records, whatever they are, are almost certainly here, since his ledger is. Now that we know that, we can wait until tomorrow to see the rest, can't we?"

Well, yes, she could wait, but Hope didn't have to like it. In the car on the way back to Los Angeles, she read the ledger in the dim glow of the map light, savoring each word.

They were nearly at Sean's house when she closed the ledger and looked over at him.

"How could he afford to do it, Sean? He sent so much money to Mexico, thousands and thousands of dollars. Didn't he need to keep some of it to live on?"

Sean glanced at her and chuckled. "Didn't you know? Whitey was filthy rich long before he ever started making movies."

"Really? I thought he made his money in films."

Sean shook his head. "My grandfather was a meat packer in Chicago. He left Whitey a small fortune. When Whitey came to California he invested in real estate and turned that small fortune into a big fortune. He started his production company with part of that fortune, but all his life, the bulk of his money was in real estate, not movies."

"How strange. It's only the movies that you think of when you think of him."

"That's how he wanted it. He liked that moviemaker's limelight, and even though he was a genius at it, he always thought real estate was boring. He wanted to be remembered for movies, not housing developments in the Valley."

"He took a tremendous risk," Hope said quietly, "dealing with Philip Carruthers. He could have been blacklisted for even that thin a connection. He could have lost everything that meant so much to him."

"He must have known what he was doing," Sean told her. "He must have thought it was worth it."

"He was a friend, that's all," Hope murmured. "He was a true friend."

Chapter 13

While they were stopped at an intersection, waiting for the traffic light to change, Sean turned to Hope. "Do you want to go back to your place? Or will you come home with me for tonight?"

Hope looked up at him quickly, then flushed and looked away. "I—I don't know," she whispered, and Sean reached over to take her hand.

"Don't be embarrassed. Please don't ever be embarrassed with me." He waited until she looked up at him again. "I didn't mean to make you feel awkward. It's just that it's late, and you have your overnight stuff with you, and this way you might get a little more sleep."

Hope bit her lip and turned her hand in his to clasp it warmly. Her smile was shy, but her soft voice was steady as she told him, "Yes, and this way I will be with you."

Sean looked into her eyes for a moment, then as the light changed and he drove on, he lifted her hand to his lips and kissed her palm. With her hand in his, resting on his thigh, he drove the rest of the way home.

They walked hand in hand to Sean's room, dropped their overnight bags inside the door and slid into each other's arms with the sense of coming home to the only place they wished to be. Hope knew that for her, at least, there was no home but Sean's embrace, and if she was parted from him, she would find that sense of rightness and security nowhere else.

She was oblivious to the luxury of the opulent bedroom suite, unaware of anything but Sean as he undressed her in the shaft of moonlight that poured through a gap in the shutters that covered the full-length windows. She felt like a goddess carved in marble, but surely no cool marble goddess could experience the pleasure of his caresses, his kisses, of the lovemaking that stripped her of shyness or feelings of inadequacy, that sent her soaring on a wave of ecstasy and brought her gently down to earth again to sleep, exhausted, in his arms.

"Hope?"

The query was soft-voiced, gentle.

"Mmm?" She snuggled closer to Sean's warmth, burying her face in the pillow.

"What time do you usually get up for work?" The second question was as gently spoken as the first.

"Six-thirty," she mumbled. "Why?"

"Because it's 7:23 right now."

There was a moment's complete silence.

"What?" she asked.

"It's 7:23."

Hope shot bolt upright in bed, clutching the bedclothes to her breasts.

"Seven twenty-three?" She scrambled off the bed, clutching a sheet around her. "Sean, I have to be at school at *eight!"*

"Fine." He rolled off the other side of the bed, magnificently unconcerned by his nakedness. "You jump in the shower, I'll make coffee, and we'll get you there on time." He waved her toward the bath. "Go on, get moving!"

She got. Hope wouldn't have believed it possible, but less than fifteen minutes after she'd awakened, Sean was driving down the canyon at breakneck speed, while Hope gulped a cup of coffee and tried to brush her hair dry in the breeze from her open window.

"I'll try to sort the stuff from the safe this morning, okay? Then when you get home from school we can go over anything concerning your father without having to wade through any more of Whitey's Mickey Mouse memos."

"All right," Hope agreed a little wistfully. "I wish I could help you sort it."

"You won't miss much," he assured her. "Just the dirty work of separating the wheat from the chaff."

"I only hope there is some wheat—besides the ledger, that is."

"With the ledger and your story, there's already enough for a movie of the week. Anything else that turns up is gravy." Sean braked to a stop in front of the school. "I'll pick you up at four. If anyone asks, just say your car's in the shop."

"Which it is," Hope pointed out.

"Which it is. I'm just the friend who helped you out, right?"

Hope didn't answer that. He was a friend, he was helping her out, but he was so much more. He was her lover, he was the man she loved. When he leaned toward her to kiss her goodbye, she surprised herself as much as him with the fervor of her kiss. He released her slowly, his gaze lingering on her lips, then touched her mouth lightly with a fingertip.

"Take care of yourself, okay?"

She nodded, hardly trusting herself to speak, then slipped out of the car and ran lightly up the steps to the school's heavy doors, smiling.

She telephoned him at lunchtime.

"Hello?" The ringing phone jerked him out of some unpalatable thoughts, and his greeting was abrupt, almost curt.

"Hello, Sean. It's me."

"Hope?"

"Mmm-hmm."

"Is something wrong?" he asked sharply. "Are you all right?"

"Oh, yes. Everything's fine."

"Oh. I wondered, since you've never called me at noon before. What's up?"

"Nothing, actually." She smiled, cradling the receiver against her cheek. "I just wanted to say hello. And to thank you for getting me to school on time this morning."

His chuckle was rueful. "I'd feel more like I deserved your thanks if I'd remembered to set the alarm last night."

"You came through in a pinch. That's more important."

"Well, thanks, even though I don't deserve it." There was a pause, and Sean cleared his throat. "Was that all you wanted?"

"Yes," she admitted, "that was all. I've been dying to know, though, how the sorting is going."

"It's going. Actually, I'm kind of in the middle of it...."

"I understand. I have to get back to the playground anyway. "I just wanted to say hello, and . . ." Her voice trailed off.

"Yes? What is it?"

"I love you, Sean." The words were little more than a whisper, but Sean heard them like a shout.

"Mmm," he mumbled. "I'll be there at four, Hope. At the same place?"

"Yes." Her voice was quieter, subdued. "At the front doors."

"See you then."

"Goodbye, Sean."

He took the phone away from his ear but didn't set it back in its cradle until he heard a "click" from Hope's end. He was frowning as he sat back and surveyed the neat stacks of papers he'd made on the kitchen table.

He had indeed spent the morning sorting the papers, first in confusion, then amazement. And finally, as he began to realize the significance of what he was seeing, in a jumble of emotions too complex to sort out. He frankly didn't know how he was going to explain this to Hope this afternoon. Hell, he wasn't sure how to explain it to himself!

It didn't help to see her face as she hurried down the steps that afternoon. She was flushed and happy, the world her oyster, and Sean hated to be the one who had to tell her her oyster was barren of pearls.

And she'd told him she loved him. Sean had tried to shove that thought away all afternoon, knowing all the while that the moment of confrontation was coming and that he would have to hurt Hope in the way he least wanted to. She was in for two unpleasant shocks, and he hated like hell to be the one who delivered them.

She burst into the house on the bubble of excitement that had kept her bouncing on the edge of her seat through the drive from school.

"Where is it, Sean?" She twirled in a quick circle as she waited for him to follow her through the hall, unable to contain her exuberance.

"It's in kitchen," he replied. "But, Hope, before you look at it—"

"What?" she demanded happily. "Are you going to tell me Whitey left this stuff in such a mess you couldn't straighten it out?"

"No, that's not—"

"Because if you are, don't bother. I could sort through anything, knowing we've finally found what I've been looking for!" She twirled in one last circle and vanished through the kitchen doorway.

Sean said nothing; what could he say, after all? He followed Hope to the kitchen, where she was gazing in excited anticipation at the piles arranged on the table.

"I put the scripts and the papers concerning each movie in a separate pile, then placed the piles in chronological order," he said quietly. "They'll make the most sense to you if you read them that way. This is the first one." He pointed, then handed her a ragged old envelope. "You should read this first."

"What is it?" She took the envelope in both hands, holding it gently, as something precious.

"Read it. You'll see." When she looked up at him uncertainly, Sean nodded, glad he could give her at least this much.

She opened the envelope and took out the single sheet it contained and read it through once, then a second time, with tears standing in her eyes. The paper was yellowed, the ink faded, but the document was as clear to Hope as it had been to Sean.

"I knew it was true," she whispered. "I knew it was."

Dated July 7, 1951, it was an agreement, a contract between Philip Carruthers and Whitey Baker, for Philip to send scripts to Whitey and for Whitey to sell them and send an agreed amount of the proceeds to Philip. It was written in a small, neat hand that Hope didn't recognize.

"That's my mother's handwriting," Sean told her when she asked. "They must have dictated it to her. Look at the signature and the witnessing."

Hope turned the paper over to look at the back again. The men's signatures were witnessed by their wives, Whitey's a bold, jagged slash, while Philip's signature was unsteady, with a blot on the *C*, as if his hand had been shaking. The signatures said as much as the written words about the two men's states of mind on that July day so long ago.

"Whitey took a terrible risk," Hope said quietly. "He didn't have to do that for my father. He would have been blacklisted, too, if anyone had learned of this." She looked at the agreement in her hand. "He'd have lost everything. He could even have gone to jail."

Sean shook his head, a small smile on his lips. "He wouldn't have believed *he* could go to jail. After all, he could keep that in the secret safe he had hidden in the fireplace."

"He took an awful risk, anyway, in the name of friendship. I wonder how many people would do that today."

Sean shrugged. "I don't know. Maybe more than you think."

"I feel like I should thank him for taking the risk of writing something like this down. This is the kind of concrete proof I need to take to the Writers Guild."

Sean glanced at the agreement, then gestured at the rest of the papers piled on the table. "You need to read the rest of it before you make plans to go to the guild, Hope. I'll leave you alone while you look through it. There's soda in the fridge, or I can make coffee, if you'd like."

"Soda is fine." Hope frowned. "Sean, is something wrong?"

He didn't answer directly. "You need to read the rest," was all he said. "I'll be in the living room when you're done, okay?"

"Well...all right." She looked at him uncertainly, then turned to the first of the chronologically arranged piles.

Sean walked out of the kitchen and went to the living room to wait.

The very first script Philip ever sent Whitey was there, on top of the first pile. It was dated December 1951, and directly beneath it was a copy of the shooting script, essentially unchanged from the original. There were some notes scribbled in the margins in Whitey's handwriting and some memos to members of the production company paper-clipped to it, along with a brief, cryptic notation that Hope recognized as referring to pages in the ledger. There was even, at the bottom of that first pile, a couple of letters from Philip in their bad-weather-fishing-boat code.

She was smiling through her tears as she turned to the second pile, but her smile soon faded, and she read on with a growing sense of grief and helpless anger.

That first script had been a good one. The film made of it had been a box office smash, the product of Philip's writing and Whitey's sage production in hiring excellent actors and a "new" director, who'd been, in 1952, at the beginning of a brilliant career.

The film made from the second script had been a winner, too, but when Hope read that script, in openmouthed astonishment, she couldn't see why. The second script, sent to Whitey just over a year after the flight to Mexico, was not great, like the first. It wasn't even good, and the shooting script gave proof of massive rewriting of Philip's idea.

By the third and fourth scripts, there was little relation at all between what Philip had written and the film that was ultimately made. Philip's scripts were ragged, with incoherent plots, rambling dialogue and occasional vague diatribes against Joe McCarthy and the political climate in the United States. There was not, she saw as she read on, a salable, much less a shootable, script in the bunch.

Yet with each of Philip's pathetic efforts, there was a shooting script and a reference to the ledger and its record of payments sent to Mexico. But they were payments, she realized, for virtually nothing. Whitey had rewritten each of those scripts, or to be more accurate, he'd written them from scratch, using what could be salvaged from Philip's work, which was sometimes as little as Philip's character names or his setting or title.

Whitey had written the scripts.

Not Philip.

Whitey had written the scripts but had still sent the money to Philip. He had kept Philip believing that his work was good, that it was being produced, that he was supporting his family. Hope even found some letters that made it clear that Whitey blamed any changes Philip might notice in the films on the moviemaking process of creativity by committee.

She didn't go looking for Sean when she finished reading, but sat at the table while the kitchen grew dark around her. There were tears in her eyes, but she was too numb to cry, too shocked even to think what to do next.

When she heard Sean's footsteps in the hall, she turned her face away, swiping at the tears with a tissue. The lights flashed on when he pressed the switch, and she turned slowly back to face him, her head lifted proudly, her eyes bleak.

He looked from her to the papers. "You've read them?"

She nodded, once. "Yes."

"I'm sorry, Hope."

"No." She shook her head almost angrily. "Don't be sorry. What your father did... It goes beyond friendship. He was a great man, Sean. He was unbelievably generous."

"I told you—he had tons of money. Whitey was always generous with money. It didn't mean anything to him."

"That's not what I meant. He was generous with money, yes. My God, he supported my family for over thirty years! But he was generous with himself, with his support. He could have told Philip that the scripts were no good. He could have let that money be overt charity, instead of calling it payment for services rendered. He could have destroyed Philip's pride, could have

taken away from him the one thing he had left, his belief in his career. It would certainly have been easier
than writing viable scripts to go with Philip's character
names or his location. He didn't have to do that. He did
it out of friendship."

"He did it because he wanted to," Sean said.
"Whitey never did anything in his life that he didn't
want to."

"Then he must have wanted very badly to be a true
friend. This goes far beyond what most so-called
'friends' would do."

They were both silent for several minutes, lost in their
own thoughts.

"Hope?"

She jumped a little, startled out of her reverie.
"Yes?"

"I don't know if you can tell me this, and don't answer if you don't want to, but didn't your father know
the scripts were rewritten? You told me that he saw the
movies when they got to Mexico. He must have realized that they were nothing like what he wrote."

"I don't know that he did," she replied slowly. "I
told you he was ill."

Sean nodded.

"Well, it wasn't just physical illness, though that was
part of it. He had what psychiatrists call bipolar disorder, what used to be known as manic-depressive illness."

"So he had mood swings?"

"Yes, but it's much more than that. It's an actual
physiological imbalance in the body that affects the
brain. When he was in a manic phase, he would have an
almost frightening energy. Sometimes he could go for
days at a time on no sleep at all, writing and writing.

But other times things would go wrong. He might experience grandiose delusions, or he might become psychotic, hallucinating. In a depressive phase, he could experience hallucinations and psychosis, as well as terrible depression and suicidal feelings.''

"Good God, Hope, how did you cope with that?" Sean slid onto the chair beside her, wrapping an arm protectively around her shoulders.

She shrugged. "He was my father. I had to cope, so I coped. When I was young, his illness wasn't so bad, and I had the help of a psychiatrist at the hospital he went to, as well. Dr. Ramirez helped me to understand both the illness and how to deal with it."

"You're very brave."

Hope disagreed. "No, I'm not. And as far as my father's knowledge of what Whitey did, looking back at things, I don't think he realized. I think he honestly believed he was responsible for those great movies, and I think his illness is the reason."

"How's that?"

"He did his writing in the manic periods. In the depressive periods he couldn't summon up the energy. He also went to see the movies during the manic periods or during the lucid periods between episodes of illness. When he was depressed he didn't leave the house."

"So when he saw the movies, he might have been having those grandiose delusions, you mentioned...."

"Or his mind was clear, but he couldn't remember what he'd written during a manic period. If he believed that what he saw onscreen was Philip Carruthers's work, and he did, then even Philip might not know otherwise."

"But if he couldn't write well because or i... how did he manage to do so well before he was blacklisted?"

"His illness wasn't so bad then. I asked Dr. Ramirez about that one time when Father was in the hospital. He said that the stability of a familiar environment, the knowledge that he was respected, his work appreciated, even my mother's support, would all have combined to help him cope better with the illness. He didn't become really sick until those supports were withdrawn one by one. That would be enough to cause problems for someone with a normal mental state. For somebody as fragile as Father, all the losses were devastating."

"But still you believed that he'd written all those films?"

"I wanted to believe. I *had* to, don't you see?" Hope pushed herself to her feet and walked a few quick paces across the kitchen, Sean following her more slowly. "And I was in the same position he was, you know. I had no reason to know differently."

"Until now."

"Until now." She looked at the papers spread over the table, and tears welled in her eyes again. "I feel as if I should have known, though. I knew what he was like, how sick he was, but I believed him when he said he'd written something wonderful. I should have known better. I should have known he wasn't capable of work like that."

"Don't blame yourself, for God's sake!" Sean took her shoulders and gave her a gentle shake. "You loved him, and you grew up knowing that your father wrote great movies. What else were you to believe?"

...w. She shook her head helplessly, and
...ars spilled over. "Thank God he never knew
...," she whispered. "It would, literally, have
...im."

"I'm glad Whitey did what he did, then."

"Oh, so am I," she said quickly. "Don't ever think
I'm not. It's just...what do I do now?"

"Do you mean about the guild and the writer's cred-
its for your father?"

"I don't know what to do." She pulled out of his
embrace and turned away, folding her arms protectively across her breasts. "I meant to glorify his memory, not tarnish it. I can't go to the guild simply to make
public how sick Father was. He knew he was ill, but he
absolutely hated to admit it. He pretended Dr. Ramirez
only came to our house to play chess with him. He never
wanted anyone to know he was ill."

"You don't have to go to the guild at all."

"But what about the first script, *The Centurion*? He
did write that, and it's a magnificent movie! Shouldn't
I go to them with that one, at least?"

Sean shook his head. "That's up to you to decide,
Hope."

"But I don't know what to decide!" she burst out in
frustration. "If I go to them with evidence of the arrangement and claim that Philip Carruthers wrote *The
Centurion* and that Whitey Baker sold it for him,
they're bound to wonder about Whitey's other films.
They might reach the conclusion that Father wrote all
of Whitey's movies." She spun around. "I can't glorify my father's memory at the expense of yours! Especially not after what he did for Father!"

"You don't have to do anything—" Sean began, but
she ignored him.

"But if I say nothing, my father's reputation remains as it is, and so does your father's, and no one will ever know what a great man Whitey Baker was. He deserves to have the truth told about him, but if that's told, then the story of Father's illness will have to be told, as well." She turned back to Sean, hands outstretched, appealing for help. "I don't know what to do!"

"I'm sorry, Hope. I can't help you."

"I love you, Sean. Please help me!"

"No." His refusal was flat, absolute. "I know you say you love me, and I care about you, too. But I didn't ask for you to love me, Hope, and I don't owe you a return on that love."

"Sean, that's not what I mea—"

"I told you not to love me. I told you I'd hurt you, even if I didn't want to or mean to. I'm sorry it hurts, Hope, but you can't ask me to make your decision for you, even in the name of love."

Chapter 14

"All right," Hope said, struggling to hide her hurt.
"If you won't, or can't, help me make my decision,
what about your decision?"

"Which decision is that?"

"Will you write about the agreement in your father's biography? Will you tell the world about him and
about Philip Carruthers?"

After a moment's silence, Sean looked across the
room at her, his eyes very dark and unreadable. "I
haven't considered that yet. I haven't made a decision."

"But as his biographer, don't you have an obligation
to tell the truth?" she demanded. "Aren't you required to tell everything you know."

"I'm only *required* not to say anything I know to be
untrue," Sean retorted. "I may choose what to include
as I see fit."

"So—" Hope returned his cool gaze "—will you choose to include the story of the agreement?"

He shrugged. "I don't know. I'm still trying to assimilate all this. Until you found those pictures of our fathers together, I really didn't believe any of this was possible. Even after you found the pictures, I wanted to keep searching primarily to prove to you that we'd done a thorough search. I didn't think we'd find anything. I certainly never thought we'd find anything like this!" His gesture encompassed the table and all that was on it. "I don't know what to think, much less what to do!"

He faced Hope, his face bland. "According to my agent, newly discovered information about Whitey is the kind of thing that would make the book a bestseller."

"Oh, wonderful! You'd exploit my father's mental illness for the sake of a bestseller? Great!"

She spun on her heel and stalked toward the doorway, only to be brought up short when Sean grabbed her arm, whirling her around and nearly yanking her off her feet.

"Damn it, Hope, wait!"

"What for?" She could hear the tears that threatened in her voice.

"Because we need to talk about this! And because I care about you!"

"Oh, come on! I told you I love you, and you made it very plain you won't let *that* inconvenient little fact have anything to do with your decision-making process! It's too late to start telling me something different!"

"Is it too late to ask you to try to calm down, to just think about all this rationally for a while? Look, Hope—" he turned her to face him, lightly holding her upper arms "—you've had too many shocks in the last couple of days, too many ups and downs. You need to take some time to think about everything."

"Don't patronize me!" Hope jerked away from him. "Don't do that to me, Sean Boudreaux, because I won't have it!" She took three quick steps along the hall, away from him. "Maybe you're right about taking time to think, though. Maybe a little time is exactly what I need." She strode away to the front door, then stopped with her hand on the knob. "And, Sean?"

"Hope, we need to talk—"

"Don't call me," she interrupted. "I'll call you... when I've made a decision."

"Did you have a good weekend in Santa Barbara?"

Sean's head snapped up, his eyes narrowing in on Don with suspicion. "Why do you ask?"

They weren't lunching on the terrace that day. They'd been driven inside by the weather, chilly and raw, with a pelting rain and gusty wind that caused shivers and turned umbrellas inside out. It was the kind of gloomy weather that often surprised winter visitors to Southern California, who expected sunshine and balmy breezes but found cold rain and snow on the mountaintops. It was the kind of gloomy weather that suited Sean's mood perfectly.

"Do I need a reason? I knew you went up there last weekend, that's all."

"Oh." Sean shrugged. "It was... it was interesting."

"Interesting? You want to expand on that?"

"No."

"Okay... Let's try another subject. Have you gotten any further with the biography of your father? You know they're anxious to see it in New York."

Sean dropped his head and ran a hand wearily around the back of his neck. "I do know, Don, but I haven't gotten much done this week. I've had a lot on my mind."

Things on his mind, like Hope.

He didn't know whether he was exasperated with her or worried about her, but he'd thought of little else since she'd stormed out of his house on Monday evening. She'd said she wanted time to think, so he'd done his damnedest to give her that time. He'd resisted the impulse to phone, he'd fought the urge to drive by her place and make sure she was all right, and he'd managed to resist the desire to go over there, take her in his arms and make love to her over and over. He'd resisted for almost four full days, but his resistance was wearing very thin. How much thinking time did she need, anyway?

"What's been on your mind?" Don asked, then smiled. "Or should I say *who* has been on your mind?"

"What are you talking about, Don?"

"Oh, come on, Sean. You and I both know the only thing on your mind is Hope."

"If she is on my mind, that's no business of yours," Sean growled.

"It is if worrying about her is keeping you from writing."

"Who says I'm worrying about her?"

"You don't exactly look like the happy bridegroom, you know. If you'd just asked her to marry you and she'd accepted your proposal, I'd expect you to be smiling."

"If I'd asked anybody to marry me, that's when I'd really be worried!"

"Don't give me that. And don't tell me you're not the marrying type, either. You had a bad marriage, and it ended. So what?"

"So I don't want to put myself or anybody else through that again, that's what!"

"Bull. You're just scared."

Sean stiffened, frowning, but Don was unimpressed.

"Hey, I was scared of taking the plunge. Any guy is. And yeah, I was nervous as hell saying 'I do', but it's the best thing I ever did in my life. If I hadn't gone ahead in spite of being scared, I'd have ended up a lonely, miserable old coot, with no one around me. I'd hate to see you end up that way, Sean."

"You don't know what you're talking about," Sean retorted. "And for your information, what was on my mind was the biography of Whitey."

"Sure it was." Don didn't bother hiding his disbelief. "But speaking of that, again, I'm really doing a lot of stalling on your behalf."

"I know. And I hate to put you in a bad position, but there's somebody I have to talk to before I can do anything more."

"Who's that?"

"That's not important. It concerns that new information about Whitey that I told you about. I've verified it, but I haven't decided whether I'm going to use it or not."

"New information is the kind of thing that sells books."

"But if it means hurting people..." was Sean's quick retort.

"That's your decision," Don told him. "I want the book to do well, Sean, but it's your book to write. Can you just give me some idea of how soon you might have something for the editor? If I can at least give her a date, that'll help her out."

Sean thought for a moment, then nodded, his decision made. "Tell her next week. I'll get the new information issue settled, one way or the other, over the weekend, and then I'll put some hard work in."

He'd given Hope the time she asked for. She'd had four days to think things over since she stormed out of his house on Monday. It was now Friday, and they were going to talk as soon as Hope got home from school, whether she wanted to or not.

Hope knew she'd behaved badly, but her emotions were in such turmoil—anger and hurt and resentment and guilt all churning around together—that she couldn't have dealt reasonably with Sean on Monday night. If she'd stayed, she'd have said things she knew she didn't mean, so it was better that she'd left. She needed time to sort herself out before she tried to sort things out with Sean.

The trouble was, four days had gone by, and she remained confused. She couldn't come to a decision about the agreement between Whitey and Philip. Should she make it known herself? Should she allow— or if it wasn't her place to give that permission, should she encourage—Sean to write about the agreement in his book?

The emotional roller coaster of the weekend had left her numb, floundering for certainty in a world that was suddenly far more uncertain than she had believed.

She needed to talk, but the only person she could discuss it with was Sean. He would understand her dilemma, but after the way they'd parted, she was reluctant, not to mention embarrassed, to go back and ask him for help.

She might have gone on dithering if she hadn't overheard Margaret talking to one of her sixth graders during the noon recess on Friday. The weather was miserable, chill and rainy, so the children had recess in the gym, which echoed with shouts and laughter and jump-rope chant. Hope was sitting on the bleachers, keeping an eye on Tommy Chavez, when she heard Margaret and her student talking a short distance away.

"But, Sister, I *can't* go and apologize! It's embarrassing!"

"And a little embarrassment is the worst thing that could happen to you, is it, Connie?"

"I'd feel stupid," the girl muttered.

"How long have you and Nita been friends?"

"Since kindergarten."

"That's a long time. Have you and Nita ever had a fight in all that time?"

"Yeah."

"And you still stayed friends?"

"Well, yeah."

"How did you manage that?"

"We made up after the fight."

"By apologizing?"

"Uh-huh."

"Were you embarrassed?"

Connie thought about that for a minute or two. "I don't know. I don't remember."

"So even if you were embarrassed at having to apologize, you don't remember it now? All you remember is that you made up and you were friends again?"

"Yeah, I guess so."

"Well, Connie, you're almost twelve years old, and I really can't tell you what to do, but I think it would be a shame if your friendship with Nita ended because you were too embarrassed to apologize."

There was a long silence, then, "I...uh...I've gotta go, Sister. Okay?"

"That's fine, Connie. You go along."

Hope waited until Connie had loped away to the other end of the gym, leggy and graceful as a colt, then she turned to look up a few rows at Margaret.

"You're pretty smart, you know that, Sister Margaret?"

Margaret grinned. "Of course I am. They teach us smart in nun school."

"I hope Connie takes the advice you said it wasn't your place to give her," Hope said. "Because I think I will."

Margaret raised an eyebrow. "Have you come to a decision about whatever it is that's been bothering you all week?"

Hope shook her head. "Not about that. But I know who I need to talk to in order to decide. And I think, like Connie, that it's worth risking a little embarrassment for." She nodded toward the far end of the gym. "Look."

Connie had been talking earnestly to a short, pretty child with long black hair. As they watched, the shorter girl, Nita, frowned and nodded, then turned to Connie with a smile that lighted up her face like a sunrise.

"All is forgiven," murmured Margaret. "They need to learn that a little embarrassment is a small price to pay for something as important as friendship."

"We all need to learn that," Hope murmured, changing the pronoun. "We all do."

Hope drove fast when she left school, keeping a wary eye out for traffic cops. Now that she'd made her decision to face Sean, apologize and ask for his help in making her decision, she couldn't get to his house quickly enough. She'd thought of phoning to tell him she was coming, but she was afraid he'd tell her not to come. Once she was on his doorstep, he'd find it much more difficult to refuse to hear her out.

Her nervousness increased as she wound her way up the canyon, but she kept going, repeating to herself Margaret's sage advice. If she loved Sean as she said she did, what did a little embarrassment matter?

Sean managed to wait, very impatiently, until Hope had had time to get home from school. At four-thirty, he shoved himself away from the desk, where he'd gotten no work done at all, and strode through the house. He was nearly at the garage door when he heard Big Ben peal behind him.

"Damn!" He swore under his breath as he about-faced and marched back to answer the door. If this was another of the rash of magazine salesmen who'd plagued him for the last week, he was going to give him a piece of his mind before sending him packing.

The bell pealed again as Sean strode into the front hall, and he yanked the door open, snarling, "What?"

Hope's smile wobbled, but she didn't turn and run. "Hello, Sean," she said quietly.

"What are you doing here?" he demanded, then could have cursed himself as she physically flinched from the harsh words. "Hey—" He caught her hand as she stepped back and kept it in his, holding her there on the steps. "I'm sorry. I didn't mean it like it came out."

"Th-that's okay." She swallowed. "I can go if it's not a good time right now..."

"No!" He pulled her in the door and closed it behind her. "Oh, no. Come on in. It's not a bad time. Come in!" He kept her hand in his and headed into the house. "You're freezing. Do you want a cup of coffee or cocoa or something to warm you up?"

He knew he was babbling, but now that she was here, like something conjured up by his wishful imagination, he was half-afraid she'd disappear again.

"No, Sean, I don't want coffee." She tried to pull her hand free, but he gripped it more tightly.

"You need something to warm up," he insisted. "Brandy?"

"No. Thank you." She stopped in the middle of the hall, forcing him either to stop or to let go of her hand. He stopped, and kept her hand in his. "I don't want anything to drink, thank you."

Sean looked at her face, then nodded. "All right. Nothing to drink, then. Will you come in and sit down?"

"Thank you." She let him show her into the living room, where she sat on one end of a sofa and Sean on the other.

They sat in silence while several seconds ticked past.

"Hope?"

"Yes?"

"Why have you come?"

She dropped her gaze to her lap. "I came because..." She hesitated, then blurted it out. "I came to apologize."

"Apologize? What for?"

"For the things I said. For stomping out of here that way. I behaved very badly, and I'm sorry."

"You don't have any reason to be sorry. I acted like a jerk. I'm the one who should be sorry."

Hope began to smile, just a little. "We could probably turn this into a long, involved argument about who's sorrier than who, couldn't we?"

Sean chuckled. "Let's don't and say we did." He leaned back, letting some of the tension ease out of his posture. "And now that we've established that we're both sorry, can I tell you something?"

"Of course."

"The reason I was ready to chew out whoever was on the other side of the door was because I was on my way to see you."

"You were?" Hope stared. "Why?"

"Why were you coming to see me?" he countered. "Apart from wanting to apologize, that is."

"I—" She stopped, took a moment to collect herself, then took a deep breath. "I need to talk to you about the agreement."

"What about it?"

"I don't know what to do. I've tried to sort it out myself and come to some kind of decision, but I can't do it by myself. I need to talk to somebody about it, but there's no one I can talk with about this except you."

"Because I'm involved, too?" he asked, unsmiling.

She shook her head and sought to explain. "Not just that, although who else would even believe this, much less understand? It's that, but it's also that I trust you."

Sean had been studying the pattern in the upholstery, but his gaze snapped up to her face at that. "Trust me? In what way?"

"You won't lie to me. You won't tell me one thing and mean another. And you understand the problem." She stopped, looked away, then asked without turning back, "Why were you coming to see me, Sean?"

It was Sean's turn to hesitate. "I tried to give you time to think. I waited four days, but I couldn't wait anymore. I needed to talk to you."

"What did you want to talk about?"

"The same thing. What to do with what we now know about the agreement. Should you go to the guild to credit Philip Carruthers with the script for *The Centurion,* knowing that if you do, the rest of the story will almost certainly come out? And should I include the story of the agreement in Whitey's biography? Frankly—" he reached across the cushions to take her hand in his "—I can't decide, Hope. And I've realized that I can't make that decision without you."

"But the book is yours. You're the one to decide what to write."

"To a certain extent. But the story of the agreement doesn't just concern Whitey. It concerns your father, and it concerns you. When you left on Monday, you didn't want it publicized because that would mean publicizing your father's illness. I couldn't make the decision to do that, or even not to do it, until I'd reached a decision that you agreed to."

Hope shook her head helplessly. "I know, and that's why I came to see you. I've hardly thought about anything but this, and I still don't know what to do."

"Neither do I." Sean lifted her hand and turned it over in his, stroking her fingers. "Do you think we could work it out together?"

"I don't know." Hope took her hand away and rose, walking over to the wall of windows to look out at the rapidly falling night. "It was just a week ago that we drove up there, wasn't it? It seems like years." She leaned her head against the glass. "I thought I knew what we'd find. I thought I knew what would happen, but everything has gotten so complicated since then."

"Some things are the same."

"No they're not!" She jerked around. "Nothing is the same! I could talk to you before, and now—" She bit her lip and turned away again. "Now everything is different."

"Because," Sean said slowly, "we made love?"

"Everything is changed now. Nothing is simple anymore."

"I was afraid that would happen. I knew you'd get hurt."

"I'm not sorry."

"Maybe you should be!"

Hope spun away from the window and marched back to confront him. "I'm not! I love you and I made love with you, and that's not something I'm going to be sorry about!"

Sean reached up, caught her hand and pulled her off balance, so that she collapsed onto the sofa next to him. "I never wanted to hurt you, Hope. You have to know that."

"I know. That's part of the problem. You're so busy trying not to hurt me that you won't let me be just a woman. You're still trying to make me into something

I'm not, some kind of perfect icon. Damn it, Sean! I'm not some kind of stupid symbol! I'm not perfect!''

"I know." He chuckled. "You have a hell of a temper."

"Don't laugh at me!" She felt the humiliating tears start and wiped furiously at her eyes. "Don't trivialize me! Look at me and see a woman, Sean! That's all I want." Her voice rose to an anguished plea. "All I want is just for you to see me as a real, flesh-and-blood woman!"

Chapter 15

Sean gathered her into his arms as the tears began to fall in earnest and held her close, murmuring words he hoped would comfort, wishing fiercely that he'd never had the occasion to hurt this gentle woman, to injure her fragile innocence. He wished he'd had the resolve, the willpower, to resist her sweet lips, her soft hands, her lovely body, to resist the flowering of her passionate nature.

He'd done what he'd done. It was too late now to alter the facts, but perhaps it was not too late to repair at least some of the damage he'd done.

"Don't cry, Hope," he murmured into her hair. "Please don't cry. I'm not worth it."

She pushed her face into his chest, rubbing her cheek on his shirtfront. "You are," she muttered. "You're kind and gentle, and you're a brilliant writer."

He disagreed. "I'm not brilliant. Whitey was brilliant. I'm an adequate journeyman writer."

"No." She leaned back and looked up at him, her lashes wet with tears, her eyes deep emerald green with emotion. "I've read what you've written, your articles and things. You're a genius at making something complicated understandable."

"You've read my stuff?" He searched her face. "But you never asked to see anything of mine."

"I got it from the library," she admitted. "I've read everything I could find. They even borrowed some things on library loan for me from the UCLA library."

"I can't believe it!" Sean pulled her close again for a hard hug. "I didn't think you'd be interested in that stuff."

"I didn't want to seem pushy, asking if I could read your work."

"Don't you know—" he lifted her face from his chest with gentle fingertips "—that there's nothing you can't ask me?"

He bent his head the fraction needed to reach her lips and let all his pent-up worry and concern flow into the kiss, all the feelings he didn't want to admit to, all the remembered passion that he'd tried so hard to deny.

Hope drew back a little when he broke the kiss, searching his face. She reached up to kiss him, quickly, then moved away.

"Hope..." He stretched an arm toward her, but she scooted back on the cushions.

"No. Let me say this." She swallowed hard and rubbed her cheeks, scrubbing away the tears. "I know that you are kind and gentle and honorable, and when I asked you to help me, you did more for me than I had any right to ever expect."

"Don't make me out to be a saint, Hope. Because I'm n—"

"But there are two things I can't ask you," she interrupted, looking straight into his eyes. "I can't ask you to suppress the truth of what happened between our fathers."

"What are you saying?"

"I want you to write the truth in your biography. The world thinks they know what kind of man Whitey Baker was. Say his name and people think of big movies and Oscars, of the flash and the glitter and the Big Ben doorbell. They think of the five wives and they snicker and think that he was a moviemaking genius, but as a person...? The world should know what kind of person he was, Sean. The world should know what kind of friend Whitey Baker was, what he did for his friend Philip Carruthers."

"You realize that will involve telling the world what happened to Philip, don't you?" Sean asked.

She nodded slowly. "Yes, I do. And that's the problem that gave me so much trouble. That is, until I realized that I was looking at it all from a very selfish point of view."

"Hope, that's ridiculous! The last thing you've been is selfish!"

"That's not true. I've been very selfish. All that talk about Father not wanting his illness publicized, that was silly! I didn't want it publicized, but I don't really think he'd have felt he had to hide it away like a dirty secret."

"What would he have wanted, then?"

"I can't be sure, but I think he'd have wanted to shed some light on bipolar disorder. People might be less inclined to treat the mentally ill as freaks if they know more about the illnesses. It was only my own cowardice that made me want to keep it a secret."

"But since you're the one who will have to face whatever publicity this generates, shouldn't it be your feelings that prevail?"

She shook her head. "Not necessarily. This is too important to conceal. What happened forty years ago has been all but forgotten. It's important to remind people what can happen, even in our 'enlightened' democracy. Hundreds of lives and careers were destroyed, but what can really bring the tragedy home to the public is the story of one individual."

"And you think Philip Carruthers's story can do that?"

"I know it can! Think of all that was lost, Sean. Father lost his career, his reputation, his home and finally his native country." She paused, thinking. "In a way, I think it cost him his mental health, too."

"I thought his illness was a result of a chemical imbalance in his body."

"It was, but stress worsened it. Can you imagine anything more stressful than being blacklisted, pilloried in the press and finally being convinced you'd been driven from your country?"

"I don't think I can imagine anything more stressful."

She nodded. "That's right. He would still have been ill if the blacklist had never happened, but who's to say that his illness might not have been less severe? And what about what the world lost?"

"The talent of all those people whose careers were ruined?"

"Mmm-hmm. Father did write *The Centurion,* and it won several Oscars. We'll never know what other works he might have given the world if he'd been allowed to live and work in peace."

"I see what you're saying, but I can't help worrying, Hope."

"About what?"

"About you. What kind of media pressure will you get when all this breaks? It's going to be a big story, make no mistake. The press will find you, and they'll demand to talk to you. Can you handle that?"

She sighed. "I've told you and told you that I'm not fragile, but you still don't believe it."

"I'm not sure you know what you're getting into," Sean insisted stubbornly. "I had to sneak in and out of the hospital while Whitey was there, and as soon as he died they were all over this house, my old place, the hospital *and* my agent's office! It was two weeks before they finally let up on me, and that was only after they'd shown the same collection of film clips of Whitey's career about eight zillion times, followed by yours truly leaving the hospital forty-five minutes after he'd died." She gasped at the callousness of that, and he nodded grimly. "They're not kind, Hope, and they couldn't care less about your feelings. If they can get a shot of you crying or shouting or being hysterical, they'll show it, again and again and again."

"I've grieved for my father, Sean. I'm not in the same emotional state anymore."

"I hope you're not. In your case, it's going to happen more than once, you know. The story will break as soon as we go to the guild to change the credit for *The Centurion,* and it'll be dredged up again when the book comes out in a year or so."

"I understand. But don't you see, in a way that's all to the good."

"How do you figure that being hounded by the press is good?"

"Because it will make people think. Father's career was destroyed, his life ruined by the witch-hunts. Your father took risks that could have destroyed him, as well. If the facts are brought before the public, not just once but two or more times, if people are reminded of the damage that kind of unchecked power can do, won't that be worth you and me having to put up with some press interest?"

Sean raised an eyebrow thoughtfully. "I think it's a story worth telling, yes. I just want to make sure you understand what will happen once it's told."

"I think I do. As well as I can before I experience it, at any rate."

"And you still want to go through with it?" he asked. "Once I send the outline to my publisher, once we take the evidence to the guild to credit Philip with his film, there will be no going back."

"I know that."

"I hope you do. Just remember, Hope, it's easy to let the tiger out of his cage, but once he's out, it's damned hard to put him back in again."

She half smiled. "Is that some bit of ancient oriental wisdom?"

He shrugged, chuckling. "I don't know where it came from, to tell you the truth. It's something Whitey said once, I think when he'd let his fourth wife see his lawyer's idea of a divorce settlement."

"I see." She laughed, then sobered. "I think this tiger needs to be out of his cage, Sean. The world should know how dangerous this tiger can be."

"All right. Can you wait until next week to go to the guild? That will give me time to write a press release on it, so you and I don't have to answer the same questions over and over. That's a lesson I learned too late when Whitey died.''

"All right," Hope agreed. "We need time to get the papers organized before we go to the guild, anyway. I suppose we can work on that over the weekend?"

"Sure. Whenever your schedule allows."

She shrugged. "You know what my schedule is. It's utterly predictable. Busy during school hours, empty on the weekends." She rose and picked up her purse. "I'll come over here tomorrow about noon, if that's all right with you."

"Noon tomorrow is fine. But wait a minute!" Sean followed as she started for the door. "Where are you going?"

"Home." She kept walking. "It's been, if you'll forgive the cliché, a long week."

"Hope!" He caught up with her and caught her arm as she pulled open the front door. "Hang on a minute!"

She looked pointedly down at his hand on her arm, and with a grimace, he released her.

"All right, Sean," she sighed. "What is it? I'm tired, and I'd really like to get home and get some sleep."

"I won't keep you long," he assured her. "There's just one thing."

"What?"

"There was something else. A second thing you said you couldn't ask me."

"Oh." Hope's eyes widened in alarm.

"What was that second thing, Hope?"

She stepped outside, onto the front steps, and lifted her chin proudly as she turned to face him. "I can't ask you to love me," she said coolly. "I realized that over the last couple of days. I can't ask for love. All I can do is tell you how I feel, and accept that whatever you feel for me is not the same." She took another step away from him. "I have no right to ask or expect you to feel something you don't feel, Sean. And I won't do that, ever again."

She started down the steps, into the rainy night, but paused and looked back from the bottom. "Good night, Sean."

He lifted a hand but said nothing as she ran through the rain to the BMW and drove off down the hill. There was really nothing he could say, was there? Hope had said it all, and quite eloquently.

And he felt like a heel.

"Miss Carruthers!" A young man with a video camera on his shoulder walked backward in front of them, and the well-dressed woman who'd shouted pushed a microphone in Hope's face as she walked down the steps from the Writers Guild offices after their second meeting there. At the first meeting, she and Sean had presented their evidence and told their story. This second meeting, a week later, had been held to officially change the credit for the script of *The Centurion* and to announce it to the press.

"Miss Carruthers, can you tell us what your meeting was about here today?"

Hope smiled coolly. "You'll find that information in the press release Mr. Boudreaux prepared."

"That's good." Sean bent briefly to whisper the commendation in her ear. "Very good."

"Mr. Boudreaux, when did you learn of the arrangement between your father and Miss Carruthers's father?"

"Recently, but you'll find that information in the press release, as well." Sean had a secure grip on Hope's arm and kept her moving steadily toward the street and his car.

"Miss Carruthers, have you seen this afternoon's headline in the *Hollywood Reporter*?"

Hope's steps slowed momentarily, but Sean urged her on. "Don't stop!" he hissed in her ear. "If you stop we'll never make it to the car!"

"No, I haven't!" Hope replied as blandly as she could. "I'm sure I will, though."

"Did you really grow up in a convent?" someone shouted.

"Was your father in an insane asylum?"

"Did he use drugs?"

"Keep walking, and keep smiling!" Sean picked up the pace until Hope was moving about as briskly as one could in heels.

He opened the car door and inserted her into the passenger seat in one smooth movement, then strode rapidly around to drop into the driver's seat and slam the door. The car was quickly surrounded by reporters, but when he gunned the powerful engine with a roar and let the machine creep forward a few inches, those in the car's path suddenly saw discretion as the better part of valor. They parted, not unlike the Red Sea before Charlton Heston, and Sean drove quickly away.

Hope glanced back at the microphone and camera-waving crowd and gave a long, shuddering sigh of relief. Sean reached across and took her hand, holding it firmly in his.

"Your hand's like ice. Is it nerves?"

"Probably," she admitted. "I'm still shaking."

"Well, you can relax now. You handled them beautifully."

"I didn't *handle* them at all! The most I did was cope."

"Then you *coped* beautifully." He signaled and turned a corner, then stomped on the gas and shot down the block and into an alley with a squeal of protest from his tires.

"What are you *doing?*" Her safety belt was the only thing that had kept Hope in her seat, and she hung on to the door handle as she demanded an explanation.

"Somebody was following us."

"*Following* us?" Hope snapped around in her seat to stare furiously out the back window. "Why would they follow us?"

"To scoop the competition," Sean told her dryly. He pulled into a space marked Private behind an office building and then back out, facing back the way he'd come. "We'll wait a few minutes before we go, okay?"

"Don't ask me. I have no experience whatever, being followed by reporters."

Sean grinned companionably. "Kind of a strange experience, isn't it?"

"Positively surreal," she agreed.

"I have a little surreality for you, I'm afraid. I don't think you should go home today."

"They'll be there, too?" She sounded more resigned than surprised."

"Oh, yeah. They'll show up at your school before this is over, too. Did you talk to the principal about it?"

"Yes." Hope smiled, remembering. "You haven't met Sister Eugenia, but if you can picture a bulldog in a veil, you've got her. I could swear she's looking forward to a confrontation with the press."

"I'll have to meet her when all this quiets down."
Sean edged the car forward, peering ahead to see if there
were any suspicious-looking cars out on the street. Satisfied that there were none, he pulled out and drove in
the wrong direction.

"Uh, Sean?" Hope asked after a few moments.

"Hmm?"

"Where are we going?"

"To my house."

"But the road to your house is back that way." She
pointed over her shoulder.

"We're going up the next canyon. The guy whose
property backs up to mine let me park in his drive and
walk over the hill to the house after Whitey died. The
reporters will be waiting down by my drive."

"Where you locked the gates this morning, right?"

"That's it exactly." He grinned. "And it would take
a brave soul to climb that hillside with all the prickly
pear on it. That stuff's better than an electrified fence
at keeping intruders out."

"Nature's security fence, I suppose. There was
prickly pear growing all along the back fence of the
convent property. Nobody ever broke in that way, but
we'd pick the fruit to eat sometimes."

"Carefully, I bet," he observed.

"Very carefully. Those spines hurt!"

"Precisely. So we'll park at my neighbor's house and
walk over the hill."

Which they did. Hope found the path over the hill
steep but navigable, even in high heels, but still she
breathed a sigh of relief when they entered the house
through the back door and she could slip her shoes off
and let the cool tile of the kitchen floor soothe her aching feet.

"Better?" Sean looked down at her feet and smiled.

"Much, thank you." Hope wiggled her toes. "Sean?"

"Yeah?" He rummaged in the refrigerator and emerged with two cans of soda.

"When will I be able to go home?"

"To tell you the truth, I don't know. Probably in a couple of days. It's a good thing your Christmas break started last Friday, isn't it?"

"It certainly is." She took the can of soda he handed her and sank onto a chair at the kitchen table. "This is crazy! I can't believe I've actually been run out of my home by a bunch of reporters!"

"Did you think all those stories about the paparazzi were made up?"

"I guess I thought they were exaggerated."

"Unfortunately not." He drank thirstily of his soda. "Good thing I stocked up on food. If we ordered a pizza, they'd all follow the delivery boy up the drive."

Behind him, the phone rang shrilly, startling Hope. Though she jumped, Sean didn't even look around. It rang again and again.

"Aren't you going to answer it?" she asked.

He shook his head. "The machine will get it. If I answer it and it's a reporter, they'll know somebody's here. I'll screen calls until this dies down."

The answering machine clicked, playing its message tape, and then they heard, "Mr. Boudreaux, this is Jim Cooper from KDBY, channel eight. I'd like to talk to you about your father and his screenplays when you get in. Give me a call. My number's 555-2296, anytime, day or night. Thanks!" The reporter hung up, and then almost immediately, the phone rang again.

"Sean, it's Don. Did you know the crowd at the end of your driveway has traffic backed up all the way down the canyon? How long do you suppose the news hounds will stay camped out down—" Sean picked up the receiver, cutting off the answering machine, and Hope could hear no more.

"Hi, Don." Sean glanced at Hope, who looked out the window and tried not to eavesdrop. "Yeah. Climbed over the hill from Charlie's driveway—007, I know. They'll give up and go away, eventually." There was a pause as he listened to something Don was saying. "Yes, she's here." He glanced at Hope, who met his eyes, then looked outside again. "Yeah. Until things settle down, anyway. Yes, Don." He sighed heavily. "Yes, I remember what you said. If I'm a coward, Don, that's my business, isn't it? Then I'll go to hell in my own way. But it's not up to you, is it? Thanks a lot, Don. You're a pal!"

He banged the receiver back onto the rest with a muttered curse.

"Is something wrong?" Hope turned back from the window.

"No." Sean shook his head. "Don's just being a busybody. He really called to see if we made it back here."

"Why does he think you're a coward?" She asked it in all innocence, merely curious, but the flush that suffused Sean's neck and cheeks showed her she'd hit a nerve she hadn't even known was there. "Sean, I'm sorry—I didn't mean to pry. If it's none of my business, just tell me so."

"You're not prying, you're just wondering." Shaking his head, Sean turned away to drop his empty soda can in the recycling box. "But it's nothing for you to—" He broke off.

Hope looked at him, standing oddly still, his broad back to her, tension visible in the rigid line of his shoulders and neck.

"Sean?" She rose slowly from her chair. "Is everything all right?"

"All right?" He shook his shoulders, easing some of the tension from them. "Yeah, I am all right." He turned around slowly. "I may be all right for the first time in a long time. You know what Don said, about my being a coward?"

"No, actually I don't." Hope frowned, puzzled. "He didn't say it to me, he said it to you."

"Yeah. But I don't think I'm going to be a coward anymore." Sean straightened to his full height. "Hope?"

"Yes?" She watched his face and waited, and her heart began to pound in quick, heavy thumps.

"Will you marry me?"

Chapter 16

There was a moment of absolute silence. Hope cleared her throat and pushed the hair back off her face.

"What . . . did you say?"

Sean jammed his hands in his hip pockets. "I said will you marry me?"

"That's what I thought you said." She looked down at the floor for a moment and pinched the bridge of her nose between her thumb and finger. After several seconds had ticked past, she looked up. "Why?"

"Why what?"

"Why are you asking me to marry you? A couple of weeks ago, you didn't want any part of the idea."

"I changed my mind."

"Why?"

"Damn it, Hope, can't a man change his mind?"

"About something like this?" she asked. "Not without a good reason. What's your reason, Sean?"

He glowered at her, but after a few seconds, the glower gave way to a reluctant smile. "Maybe I decided it was time to stop being a coward."

Hope rolled her eyes in exasperation. "You're talking in riddles. Would you mind telling me what this coward business is all about? In what way are you a coward?"

Sean walked back to her, slowly, a step at a time. "I have it on good authority," he said, "that I'm a coward about a very important part of life."

"What on earth are you talking about?"

He took another step closer, so that only one short pace separated them. "According to Don, who is very wise in these matters, I'm afraid of love."

He watched Hope, his smile never wavering, while her eyes widened and her face paled slightly.

"What, Hope? Nothing to say?"

"I—I didn't think that comment required an answer," she stammered.

He shrugged. "Maybe it doesn't. Don seems to find the subject endlessly fascinating, but he's a newly-wed—he's a little prejudiced on the subject."

Hope shook her head in confusion. "What subject? Cowardice?"

"No, silly. Marriage!"

"He's prejudiced about marriage? Sean, you're not making sense!"

"I'm making perfect sense, but you're not listening." Sean caught her shoulders and drew her close, so that she had to look up, into his face. "According to Don, I've been running from love because I had a bad marriage. According to Don, if I don't stop running and take a chance on happiness when it presents itself, I'll end up a lonely, bitter old man. And I've decided he just may be right. So, Hope—'' he bent his knees slightly to look directly into her face ''—will you marry me?''

Hope stared into his eyes for long seconds, seeking something, some answer she needed. She opened her mouth, then closed it again and suddenly pushed against his chest, twisting out of his grasp and stumbling backward away from him, her stockinged feet slipping on the smooth tiles.

''Hope—'' Sean reached for her, but she evaded him.

''No! The answer is no!'' She grabbed her purse and started for the stairs. ''I won't marry you just because your agent said something that got your goat!'' She turned and fled for the stairs. Sean followed, until she stopped on the third step up and looked over the banister at him. ''And in case you decide to ask anyone else to marry you, Sean Boudreaux, let me give you a piece of advice. Ask her because you want to live with her, because you can't live without her, *not* because someone else told you to!''

Her footsteps pounded up the stairs, along the upstairs hall, and then the guest room door slammed shut with a bang that seemed to rattle windows all through the house. Sean winced at the sound.

''Damn!'' he swore heavily. ''Damn, damn, damn!'' He plodded back to the kitchen and slumped into a chair. How could he have been so stupid, so clumsy? What the hell was he thinking of, proposing to Hope by telling her that Don told him to. No wonder she was insulted!

The question was, what did he do about it now? She was livid with him, and no wonder. But what could he do now to get her to forgive him?

There had to be something....

* * *

"Hope?" He tapped on the guest room door.

"Go away!" Her voice was muffled, as if, he thought, she'd been crying.

"Hope, I have some dinner for you. Will you just open the door so I can give it to you?"

"I'm not hungry!"

"Hope, you have to eat! Now, open the door!"

"No! Just go away!"

"I'm not going away, Hope! And if you don't open this door, I'm going to kick it in!"

There was a moment of shocked silence. "You wouldn't."

"Want to try me?" Sean set the dinner tray on a small mahogany table in the hall and stepped back, gauging the distance to the lock. "One good kick is all it'll take."

"You'll ruin the woodwork!"

"I couldn't care less about the damned woodwork!" he shouted. "You've got till three, Hope. One!" He half turned, preparing to deliver a karate kick to the doorknob. "Two!"

There was a sudden rush of movement on the other side of the door. "No!" Hope shouted. "Don't kick it! I'll open it, just give me a minute!"

There was some rattling as she fumbled with the lock, then she flung the door wide and stood aside. "Just put the food over there and get out!" she snapped.

She was wearing the terry cloth bathrobe that usually hung in the back of the door, and she stood half turned away from him, her face averted.

Sean carried the tray over to a small table by the window. Flanked by two Chippendale chairs, it served as both a writing desk and compact dining area. When he'd set the food down, though, he didn't leave.

"Go on, Sean, just get out of here!"

Hope still had her head lowered, so that her hair swung down and hid her face from him. She stood with one hand on the door, clearing waiting to slam it on his heels as he made his exit.

"No," he said almost gently. "I'm not leaving until we've talked."

"There's nothing to talk about."

"Yes, there is." Sean took her hand from the door, keeping it in his when she would have jerked away. "I insulted you, and I have to apologize. I can only say that my words weren't meant as an insult, Hope. I'm sorry."

"All right. You're sorry. Will you go now?"

"No. We still need to talk." He drew her across the room despite her resistance and seated her on the edge of the bed, then sat beside her.

Hope was steadily shaking her head. "Sean, I don't want to talk right now, not about anything!"

"You're hurting, and it's my fault." He touched her cheek and found it wet with tears. "You've been crying tears that I caused, and I can't let that go on."

"I doubt if you can stop it," she said with a watery chuckle. "I certainly can't."

"Not even if I tell you I love you?"

She went very still, then shook her head in a firm negative. "Don't do this, Sean. Don't say something you don't mean. It's too cruel."

"You're right, it would be cruel, if it wasn't true," he said quietly. "But it *is* true. It's been true for a while, but I was afraid to admit it.

Hope sniffed. "You're just saying that because your agent told you to."

"I'm saying it because I love you. And because you trusted me enough to tell me about your feelings. And because you trusted me enough to make love with me, even though I told you I was going to hurt you." He took her chin in gentle fingers and lifted it so he could see her face. "I was afraid to feel love, Hope. I was terrified to admit, even to myself, that that's what I felt for you."

"But—" She shook her head. "Why would you be afraid to admit you felt love? That doesn't make sense."

"Not to you, because love has been something good in your life, fulfilling and rewarding and mutually shared. My view of it was different. I was very idealistic when I was young, and more than a little naive, not to mention too smug to see reality. I married the wrong woman. I had great plans for that marriage, but it ended in the kind of bitterness that takes a lot of getting over. I'm not trying to make excuses for myself," he added hastily. "I was at fault for marrying for the wrong reasons, and also for letting one failure make me so gun-shy that I practically became a hermit. I have no one but myself to blame for that."

"I did know that you didn't want to get married again," she said. "But I didn't know why. And I didn't understand why you told me not to fall in love with you."

"I was scared," he admitted. "You scared me to death!"

"How could I scare you?" She swiped the terry sleeve of the bathrobe across her eyes and looked up at him.

"You were everything I knew I didn't deserve. You were innocent and good and honest and sweet. I knew perfectly well that a jaded, reclusive old cynic like me didn't deserve that kind of goodness."

She made a small sound of protest, but he laid a finger on her lips.

"Let me tell you all of it." She nodded, and he let his hand fall back into his lap. "I knew that I had nothing to offer you but hurt, but I couldn't help wanting what I couldn't have. I saw you each day, and I wished that I could have a little of what you had. I saw the love you felt for your father, and knew how much I'd missed with mine. I didn't think much of him, you know. At that time, I didn't know what he'd done for friendship.

"You showed me what I'd missed, but you also gave me so much. You gave me a knowledge of Whitey that I'd never have had if it hadn't been for you. I don't have the words to thank you for that." He lifted her hand to his lips and pressed a kiss into her palm.

"Don't thank me, please! I started this entirely to give my father the credit he didn't have while he was alive. I didn't intend to be at all generous about Whitey, except in as much as he helped my family. I was fully prepared to take away his credit for all those movies."

"But you were going to give him credit for being the kind of man who helps his friends at great personal risk. You would have enhanced his reputation, not damaged it."

"Still, I'm ashamed to say I wasn't really thinking about him at all."

"You have nothing to be ashamed of. There's plenty I wish I hadn't said or done."

"But you—"

Again he stopped her words. "I was falling in love with you, but I wouldn't admit it to myself, and I wouldn't admit it to you. Even when you told me you loved me, even when we made love, I was too afraid to tell you, and that's what I can't forgive myself. I denied you the truth. I hurt you, for no reason other than the protection of my own ego, and I won't forgive myself for that."

"You were falling in love with me?" she whispered.

"Oh, yeah. Didn't you notice that I couldn't take my eyes off you?" His chuckle was low and intimate. "I couldn't stop wondering what you wore under those floaty skirts and those lace-collared blouses. I couldn't stop wanting to take those pretty, romantic, old-fashioned clothes off you and make love to you all night long."

When he slid his arms around her, she didn't resist but nestled against him and rested her head on his shoulder.

"That weekend in Santa Barbara was like a dream," he murmured into her hair. "Like a dream I'd had that could never be reality. Coming back here was like waking up and finding that the dream didn't last, that the bad old world was back again."

"But it didn't have to be."

"I know that, now. I didn't know it then. I was still running too hard to see the happiness that was right there in front of me."

"And now?" Hope looked up, watching his face, his eyes.

"Now..." Sean looked down at her, his eyes very dark. "Now you hold my happiness in your two hands."

He slid off the bed to rest on one knee beside it, her right hand clasped in both of his. "I love you, Hope Carruthers. You are my lover, my woman, the woman I love. Will you do me the honor of becoming my wife?"

Hope felt the tears well in her eyes as she leaned down to cradle Sean's face in her hands. "I love you, Sean, and I don't want you on your knees, not ever. I love your pride as much as your kindness and your strength and the sexy way your beard gets heavy in the evening."

"My beard?" He rubbed an experimental hand over his scratchy chin and grimaced. "Guess I should have shaved, huh?"

"Not for me." Hope shook her head, her hair swinging onto his shoulder as she bent to press her lips to his cheek and then his mouth. He kissed her hungrily, sliding back up onto the bed to draw her more fully into his arms. He eased her onto his lap and kissed her again, then lifted his head.

"Will you marry me, Hope? Not because Don pointed out my lack of courage, or because you had the courage to trust when I didn't, but simply because I love you and I don't want to live my life without you?"

Hope leaned back a little, balancing herself with her hands on his upper arms. She smiled up into his eyes. "Yes."

"Yes?"

"Yes. Yes, yes, yes! Yes, I'll marry you, because I love you and you love me, and yes, I'll marry you!"

With a whoop of joy, Sean caught her as she flung her arms around his neck, and they tumbled backward together onto the bed. He rolled until he was propped on his elbows above her, and they kissed until they were breathless and beginning to ache with the familiar need.

"You know what else I've been wondering about?" Sean asked in a husky whisper. He pushed Hope's tumbled hair back from her flushed face.

"What have you been wondering?" she whispered.

"I've been wondering what you're wearing under this thing." He plucked at the lapel of the bathrobe.

"Oh." Hope's eyes widened as Sean slipped one fingertip beneath the lapel and began to ease it off her shoulder.

"I have a feeling," he murmured, "that you'll keep me wondering all our lives, won't you?"

Hope's only reply was a breathless "Oh!" as he discovered the answer to at least one of his questions.

The first copies of *Whitey: A Life in the Movies*, arrived by mail from New York. Sean opened the package, took out a copy and turned a few pages, then handed it, open, to his wife of one year. Hope read the words with tears of joy in her eyes.

This book is dedicated to Whitey Baker, a man who was more than the sum of his movies, to Philip Carruthers, who kept his pride in the face of a nation's shame, and most especially to Hope, who brought love back into my life.

* * * * *

This is the season of giving, and Silhouette proudly offers you its sixth annual Christmas collection.

SILHOUETTE

Christmas Stories

1991

Experience the joys of a holiday romance and treasure these heart-warming stories by four award-winning Silhouette authors:

Phyllis Halldorson—"A Memorable Noel"
Peggy Webb—"I Heard the Rabbits Singing"
Naomi Horton—"Dreaming of Angels"
Heather Graham Pozzessere—"The Christmas Bride"

Discover this yuletide celebration—sit back and enjoy Silhouette's Christmas gift of love.

SILHOUETTE CHRISTMAS STORIES 1991 is available in November at your favorite retail outlet, or order your copy now by sending your name, address, zip or postal code, along with a check or money order for $4.99 (please do not send cash), plus 75¢ postage and handling ($1.00 in Canada), payable to Silhouette Books, to:

In the U.S.
3010 Walden Ave.
P.O. Box 1396
Buffalo, NY 14269-1396

In Canada
P.O. Box 609
Fort Erie, Ontario
L2A 5X3

Please specify book title with your order.
Canadian residents add applicable federal and provincial taxes.

SX91